Carl Weber's Kingpins:

Houston

Carl Weber's Kingpins:

Houston

Treasure Hernandez

www.urbanbooks.net

Urban Books, LLC
300 Farmingdale Road, N.Y.-Route 109
Farmingdale, NY 11735

Carl Weber's Kingpins: Houston
Copyright © 2019 Treasure Hernandez

ISBN 13: 978-1-945855-61-0
ISBN 10: 1-945855-61-4

First Trade Paperback Printing January 2019
Printed in the United States of America

10 9 8 7 6 5 4 3 2 1

*This is a work of fiction. Any references or similarities
to actual events, real people, living or dead, or to real
locales are intended to give the novel a sense of reality.
Any similarity in other names, characters, places, and
incidents is entirely coincidental.*

Distributed by Kensington Publishing Corp.
Submit Orders to:
Customer Service
400 Hahn Road
Westminster, MD 21157-4627
Phone: 1-800-733-3000
Fax: 1-800-659-2436

Prologue

Donna gasped and gulped in a lung full of air so fast it made her cough and wheeze. Her lungs felt like someone had ignited them with gasoline and a match. "Uhhh," she panted, her head whirling around in circles as she tried to catch her breath. Her entire body quaked so hard every one of her muscles ached. She could hear faint sounds, but nothing was louder in her ears than the whoosh and pounding of her own coursing blood.

Finally, Donna forced her eyes open, but she couldn't see anything due to the blindfold covering her eyes. There were several dark figures moving around her—the source of her agony. She shivered. She was freezing. Her attackers were throwing buckets of water at her to wake her up every time she blacked out.

"Mmm, my . . . sis . . . sister?" Donna rasped through her cracked and busted lips.

"Y'all hear this? Awww, she's asking for her sister," a man with a deep voice taunted to whomever else was there.

Donna could tell there were others walking back and forth in front of her because she could hear the sound of shoes against the floor. She was tied to a chair.

"Mmmm," she groaned and attempted to move her body, but all she managed to do was cause the thick nautical ropes to cut deeper into her wrists and ankles. She shivered again. Donna had learned from her father that this was a sign of shock. She had to stay awake. She had to find her sister.

"Wh . . . what do you want?" Donna managed through her swollen lips. The pounding in her head was so bad that even moving her mouth felt like hell.

Donna could tell that the man had stopped walking, his footsteps silenced. She could also tell he was close . . . extremely close. She could smell the strong scent of his cologne mixed with his body odor. It was like he'd been sweating.

"What do I want?" the man repeated. Then he laughed raucously like she'd said something hilarious. "She wants to know what I want," he called to whomever was there with him. Then he let out another maniacal laugh that was so evil it stabbed at Donna's eardrums. She shivered again as fear gripped her tight around her throat.

"This bitch got some nerve for sure," the man spat venomously. "I guess we gon' have to show her what I want, since she so fuckin' bold to ask," he yelled.

The thunder of more than one pair of feet came fast and furious in Donna's direction. The one talking was calling the shots.

"Ugh," Donna wolfed out in agony as a punch landed to her gut. All of the air deflated from her lungs, and she felt like all of her ribs had shattered. Another forceful blow landed to her chest, sending daggers of pain through her entire torso. Donna felt pain like she'd never experienced in her life, which told her something inside of her had been shattered. Donna coughed, wheezed, and gagged as punches rained down on her face, head, back, and stomach. With the next round of blows, she felt one of her teeth shoot from between her lips. Blood spilled from her face like water spilling from a cracked coconut.

"Pl—please," Donna begged. The pain was too much to bear. "Wh—what do you . . . you want?" she gasped, asking again. They could've killed her by now.

All she wanted to know was who it was and to finally understand what they wanted. How did they get her? She couldn't remember. Donna was caught slipping.

"A'ight," the man hissed, backing off his little minions. "Now, what I want is what's been owed to be me for years. All that they took from me. All that y'all took from me," he gritted.

Donna swallowed hard. She had no idea who this man was. It could've been any one of the licks she, Donna, and Aunt Lisa had pulled over the years. It could've been old enemies of her parents. He could've been anybody. What was clear to Donna was that he wasn't going to stop until she figured it out.

"I . . . I don't know who . . . or . . . what you're—" she started, rasping out each word with strained effort. Before Donna could finish, a hard, open-handed slap landed to her face with so much force it rocked her body.

"Don't fucking lie! If you lie, you're fucking insulting me, and if you continue to fucking insult me—" he growled. He moved to Donna's side and got close to her face. He snatched off her blindfold. "This bitch will suffer longer, and she will die right in front of your fucking face." The man snatched Donna's head back and forced her to look.

"Kim! Oh my God! No! Kim!" Donna screeched, coming alive like her body wasn't wracked with pain. "Let her go! Kill me! But let her go!" Screaming hurt so bad, but Donna didn't care. "Let her fucking go! Agggh! Kim!" Donna bucked her body against the restraints so hard the thick nautical rope cut bloody, jagged lines into her skin. Seeing her sister threatened to give Donna a heart attack. Kim was naked, and blood covered her face. She looked dead. There was no movement even as Donna was screaming her name.

"Now that you can see that I'm not fucking around, maybe you'll act right," the man hissed. He put the blindfold back on Donna before she could really open her eyes. The injuries were bad, and it was getting to the point where her eyes were almost swollen shut. She groaned and bucked some more, ignoring the excruciating pain. Not being able to see Kim was killing her.

"No! Please! I need to see my sister! Please!" she pleaded, the veins in her neck and arms cording against her skin. "You motherfucker!" Donna screeched. She wasn't being nice anymore, not when it came to her sister.

The man emitted another sinister laugh. This time the sound of his laughter infuriated Donna more than it scared her.

"Kim! Kim, I'm here! Kim!" Donna screamed out until she was silenced by a punch to the mouth that filled her mouth with more sharp, metallic-tasting blood.

"Shut the fuck up!" the man boomed. "You bitches think you're untouchable! Your whole family thought they were untouchable! What made you bitches think you could get away forever?" the man asked, his mood quickly changing back to serious and his laughter turning into fury.

"It didn't matter where y'all went, moving to a fancy house off the backs of other niggas. Y'all were still ghetto trash. You know what they say: karma is a bitch, and she don't ever miss. I guess you can say I'm karma today," he spat.

Donna shook her head. "Just . . . just kill me," she croaked out. Tears danced down her cheeks. It was obvious she and Kim weren't going to make it out of this.

"That's it? You think I would let you bitches off that easily?" he snarled. "This bitch has got to be kidding me. She wants me to just kill her. Boom, kill her and put her out of her misery. Naw, misery is what I like to see, bitch," he announced loudly.

With that, another bevy of punches and slaps came down on Donna like a hailstorm. She could barely keep her head up. She couldn't breathe. She knew that a fractured rib had probably punctured one of her lungs. She was going to die, and she welcomed it. She accepted it. But she didn't want to think about her sister dying.

"Let's show her what happens to our enemies," the man instructed his goons. They snatched the blindfold off Donna's eyes again. This time, she squinted in an attempt to find Kim through the bright light shining directly on her as if she were on display. The light was painful to her eyes. It was so bright she couldn't see anything but spots. Her head pounded, and she could barely keep it up.

Finally, after a few seconds, Kim came into focus in front of Donna. She could see that Kim was injured, just like her, but Donna couldn't tell what had happened. It was hard to see anything else. Then she heard buzzing, like a saw or some kind of machine. A man walked over and put something up against Kim's naked body. The next thing Donna knew, Kim's body jerked, and she emitted a blood-curdling scream that could've cracked the thickest glass.

"Agggh!" Donna shrieked and snapped her eyes shut. "No!" She couldn't stand to watch her sister in so much pain.

The man used the machine again. This time, Donna could see that it was an industrial sandblaster.

"Please, stop! I'll do whatever you want!" Donna begged, choking on her own tears. Another slap across the face snapped her neck. Pain crashed down on Donna and threatened to knock her out. The hit landed with so much force, blood and spit shot from her lips.

"Please . . . take me. Nust let her go," Donna puffed through her swollen lips. "I'm begging. Please. She didn't do anything. Just take me," she rasped, barely able to get enough air into her lungs to get the words out.

"It doesn't matter now," the man growled evilly. "Now, watch!" He grabbed Donna's face and forced her to watch.

Kim let out another ear-shattering scream. Donna could've sworn she could hear Kim's skin shredding right off her body. Donna couldn't stand to look. They had Kim's wrists bound and her arms positioned over her head. Her face was covered in a mix of tears, snot, and blood. Her hair was soaked with sweat and matted to her head. There were marks running up and down her once flawless body. Donna knew then that even if by some miracle they made it out of there alive, Kim would have a long road of recovery ahead of her. Kim had always been the stronger one, but in Donna's eyes, she might be better off dead than scarred for life. Kim was the beauty, where Donna had always considered herself more of the brains.

Donna sobbed. She didn't know if it had been their greed that landed them there, or if it was indeed karma from their past, like her attacker had said. They had done some fucked up things over the years to get on top. Their father had done some fucked up things in his life, too. So had Aunt Lisa. Donna didn't know if it was their sins or the sins of their father biting them in that moment.

More buzzing interrupted her thoughts. More screams from her sister sent Donna's emotions into overdrive again.

"Oh my God! Kim!" Donna screeched until her throat itched. She had to try to fight for her sister. She strained against the restraints. "Kim! I'm sorry! I'm so sorry! I love you!"

Kim let out another scream. This time vomit spewed out of her mouth like a volcano. Donna could feel the warm body fluid hitting the bottoms of her legs. Donna gagged. All she could think about was that her sister was going to die and leave her with no one.

The tormentor's loud laughter sent a feeling of doom over Donna like a black cloud. There was nothing else she could say or do to get them out of this. They were about to die. And, at that point, Donna welcomed death again with open arms.

She yelped as her scalp exploded in pain. Her head was yanked up by her hair.

"Keep your fucking eyes open," a deep, scratchy voice demanded. It was a different voice this time.

Donna could feel hot breath on her face. The stench of old cigarettes and alcohol shot up her nose. She squinted her battered eyelids. The blurry image of a man's face came into focus but quickly went fuzzy again. Donna felt her heart seize a little bit. If they didn't kill her, the face in front of her was about to. She had finally met the person responsible for all of her pain.

"You're going to watch your little bitch sister die now," he growled in her face. "All y'all had to do was be loyal, but all of y'all are the same. Traitors."

Donna felt her heart sink but realized she was powerless. She opened her mouth to address the familiar voice, but she couldn't find any words. Her legs trembled fiercely. Sweat danced down her spine. She couldn't stop obsessing over the questions. How didn't they see it? Why wouldn't they know this would happen? Why didn't they figure it out from the jump?

"Kim . . . I'm sorry." Donna cried so hard her entire body rocked. She heard Kim scream one more time. It was a deep, guttural scream that Donna could imagine coming from a mother losing her child or an animal about to die. Kim gurgled a few times. And then, there was silence. The silence seemed louder to Donna than Kim's screams.

"Didn't any fucking body ever teach you how to be loyal?" the familiar voice asked. Then he pushed Donna over until her body crashed violently to the floor.

Donna didn't even care anymore. Pain and grief plunged her into darkness as her mind tried to figure out where it had all gone wrong.

Chapter 1

One Year Before

"Aunt Lisa, we know," Kim started, her voice jerky. Aunt Lisa let out a short snort and glared at her nieces, looking from one to the other. Kim looked over at her sister, Donna, for help. Donna lowered her eyes and didn't even bother to say what she was about to say.

Aunt Lisa's Christian Louboutin heels sounded off on the Italian marble floors of the mini-mansion she shared with her nieces. Kim looked up again and opened her mouth, but an eye-dagger from Aunt Lisa drove Kim's eyes to the floor, and every few seconds, she would see her aunt's feet pass her eyes. Kim and Donna weren't sure what was coming next, because Aunt Lisa, who had been their guardian since they were ten and twelve, had a serious poker face.

Aunt Lisa paced in straight lines, her shoes making the eerie sounds like a soundtrack to doomsday. Not a good sign for the girls. Over the years, Kim and Donna had witnessed their aunt's soft love, but most of all, her tough love. Aunt Lisa had raised the girls to be confident, beautiful, and sophisticated, but also stealthy and streetwise.

Now, they both watched as Aunt Lisa bit her bottom lip and continued burning holes in the floor as she moved with no real destination. Aside from her footsteps, it was so quiet they could probably hear a mouse pissing on cotton.

A loud knock at the door rattled all of them. Kim's heart started galloping like she'd just run around the block. She started chewing on her bottom lip like it was a piece of steak. Donna exhaled loudly and played it cool, but her eyes said something different.

The door rattled again. Aunt Lisa stopped moving. She stormed to the two huge, cherrywood and stained-glass doors and pulled them back tentatively. All the air seemed to rush out of the room when Keraun walked smoothly through the doorway. As usual, his facial expression was hard to read, and his swagger was on a million.

Kim swallowed hard and looked over at her sister. Donna darted her eyes from Kim to Aunt Lisa to Keraun, and then back again.

Aunt Lisa nodded at Keraun knowingly. He nodded back and looked at Kim and Donna. He smirked, since smiling wasn't something he did.

"Why y'all so tense up in here?" he asked, his smooth baritone changing the mood in the room from serious-as-cancer to almost light-as-a-feather. Kim and Donna relaxed a little bit, but they still waited for the word from Keraun and the approval of their aunt. He turned toward Aunt Lisa and tilted his head. Kim was holding her breath. Donna's eyes were closed.

"These girls ain't no joke outchea. You taught them well, Lis," Keraun announced. "Ain't nobody coulda asked them to do it any better than this. On point shit, Lis. They grew up fast . . . but good," Keraun said, his eyes falling on Kim as usual.

She shivered a little bit. Kim had loved Keraun, or King K as he was known in the streets, since she was a little girl. He wasn't as old as Aunt Lisa, but he was still much older than Kim. He was the only man directly in their lives. The girls always thought their Aunt Lisa and

Keraun were getting it in on the low, but there was never any real evidence to say that was so.

Aunt Lisa turned toward her nieces and finally, approval glinted in her beautiful, slanted hazel eyes. She winked at them. Kim's shoulder's slumped, and she blew out a windstorm of breath. Donna smiled and rubbed her hands together like an excited kid at Christmas. They were all feeling the same thing—a hella relief and a whole lot of satisfaction.

Kim and Donna had officially pulled off their lick, thanks to the teachings of Aunt Lisa and Keraun. At first, when they hadn't heard from Keraun, and Aunt Lisa looked like she wanted to take their heads off, they didn't know what to think.

Kim had been so nervous when she'd set up their latest mark, because she wasn't sure if the plan would work. She also wasn't sure the dude had fallen hard enough for her striking beauty that he hadn't done any kind of homework about her. The setup took more time than it usually did. Kim had almost lost her nerve a few times along the way. Donna had to console her and help her keep her head in the game. They took risk, but it had paid off.

One thing was for sure: neither Kim nor Donna wanted to ever let Aunt Lisa down. She had given them everything after their parents had gone missing, never to be seen again. They felt like they could never repay her.

After their parents disappeared, Aunt Lisa was there. She kept them clean, fed, and wanting nothing. Well, there was only one thing the girls wanted: their parents. Although Kim and Donna pleaded with Aunt Lisa to tell them why their parents left or where they went to, she always told them it was better this way. After a few years, Kim and Donna decided that their parents were dead and Aunt Lisa just couldn't bear to tell them the truth.

"Y'all did damned good," Keraun said, moving closer to Kim again. "You did *real* good." His voice went lower, sexier.

Kim could feel the heat from his words on the side of her face. She immediately got goosebumps. *Shit*, she thought. Kim was instantly wet and tried her damndest to hide it.

Keraun was such a smooth-operating dude. He'd been in the streets of Houston for years, and he knew all the old heads, the new niggas, and the real flashy, easy marks who, although they didn't have real money, were so easy to set up and rob they couldn't pass on them. Keraun walked and carried himself with so much swag that it was hard not to be attracted to him. Keraun always dressed impeccably. Kim and Donna had never seen him look one bit disheveled. His thick, neatly trimmed beard was never sloppy, his nails were always neatly trimmed and freshly manicured, and his sneakers were so clean they gleamed. Keraun always wore a brand spanking new Houston Rockets fitted and never repeated one. He was sharp as hell.

Keraun spent his days partnering with Aunt Lisa to teach Kim and Donna about life. He always stressed that Kim's striking beauty would ensure that Kim and Donna stayed fed, stayed rocking the best clothes, and stayed living the life of luxury that they lived now, even if he and Aunt Lisa weren't around to take care of them one day.

"I guess we taught them well," Aunt Lisa said, moving between Keraun and Kim. Aunt Lisa gave Keraun a stern, raised-eyebrow look. Keraun smiled nervously— one of the only times he allowed himself to smile. They all knew the smile wasn't actually a smile. Instead, it was Keraun's guilt about his obvious lust for Kim and the fact that he knew Aunt Lisa was super protective of her nieces.

"Well, if we did such a good job, tell us what's up," Donna said, sitting on the edge of her seat, her legs moving in and out in anticipation. Kim nodded her agreement as she eyed the big black duffle bag Keraun held. Aunt Lisa had her arms folded across her chest, but Kim and Donna knew their aunt's heart was probably thumping like crazy. The rapt anticipation in the room was palpable, to say the least.

"C'mon, Keraun. Let me see what my little protégés got done out there. Your ass know the damn suspense got my guts bubbling and shit," Aunt Lisa complained. She looked like she wanted to run up on Keraun and snatch the duffle bag.

"Your ass is beautiful when you mad," Keraun joked. He was right. Aunt Lisa had held on to her youthful beauty; she always got mistaken for Kim and Donna's sister, not their aunt.

Not only did Aunt Lisa keep her body right and in shape, but she always wore the best clothes, down to her socks and bras. Nothing Aunt Lisa wore was anything less than Gucci, Louis Vuitton, Balmain, and Chanel. She had very rich taste, and she made sure her nieces did too. Kim was the most like Aunt Lisa. She liked to follow Aunt Lisa's lead with makeup, perfume, high-end clothes, expensive bags, and shoes—lots of shoes.

"Stop fucking with me, nigga. Get the fuck down to business," Aunt Lisa said, kicking off her heels like she was getting ready to fight.

Keraun threw his hands up. "Oh, shit. Don't beat my ass now," he said, laughing.

He set down the duffle bag. Everybody in the room had their eyes on that bag. The sound of the zipper seemed so loud in Kim's ears. She didn't even realize she had been holding her breath again. Keraun stretched the top of the bag open. Everybody's eyes fell down to the same spot. Aunt Lisa was the first to react.

"Get the fuck out of here!" she yelled, clapping her hands together. "You bitches did it! I fucking love y'all!" she exclaimed excitedly.

That was everyone's signal that celebrations were in order. The stacks of money smelled like weed from being in the trap house, but they didn't give a damn. That shit looked like the most beautiful thing they had ever seen. Kim and Donna jumped up and started screaming and hugging each other. They had finally taken everything Aunt Lisa and Keraun had taught them over the years and put it to use. Together, the girls had pulled off one of the biggest licks since they had starting setting niggas up. After it was all said and done, their lick had netted them three hundred and forty-five thousand dollars. All of that money, free and fucking clear—or so they thought.

Kim hugged her sister, then Aunt Lisa, and finally Keraun. He held onto her a little longer than she expected, and secretly she loved every minute of it.

The squeals and loud laughter reverberated through the house as Kim and Donna celebrated their lick. Kim took two handfuls of cash and tossed them up in the air, letting the money rain back down over her and Donna's heads. Kim squealed with laughter, and she whirled around in the cash.

"Sissy, we caught a lick! We caught a lick! Bitch, we rich! We caught a lick!" she sang jokingly.

Donna laughed. "Over three hun'ed thousand! We just get better with time, baby sis! Next time we taking a nigga for half a mil!" Donna declared.

Kim continued to jump around. She felt like they had just hit the lottery. The girls were as happy as a faggot with a bag of dicks, as Aunt Lisa always said when she was overjoyed about anything.

"Listen! Stop all that bullshit. Y'all sound like some li'l girls in love or some shit. We can't be getting all crazy," Aunt Lisa chastised. "I know y'all happy and shit, but this how bitches get sloppy . . . let they guards down. Don't act like this the be it and be all, because if you feel like you got it all now, you won't work as hard and be as careful every time. And, remember, ain't no spending going down until shit die down. Yes, we live up in this white neighborhood, but you know how y'all is, always got one foot in the hood showing off. Calm the hell down. And I mean it," Aunt Lisa said seriously. She was blowing their high, for real.

Kim and Donna both tried in vain to simmer down and keep a serious face while Aunt Lisa was standing in front of them, but inside, they were still bursting with excitement. Aunt Lisa had spent years providing them with the very best of everything, but this was different. This was all them. It felt damned good to go out there and get their own shit.

Kim's insides were bursting with laughter, and after a while, she could no longer hold it in. She was about to explode and couldn't help but let out another round of squeals. Aunt Lisa's eyes fell into tiny dashes so small they were almost closed. She stepped over and gave Kim and Donna a serious side-eye, one that was familiar to them since childhood. It meant *Stop playing with me!* Again, the girls tried to be serious. Even Donna, the one who often played shit cool, could barely contain her smiles.

"Oh, y'all wanna play with me? Y'all think shit funny?" Aunt Lisa snapped, but before she could move closer to her nieces, Keraun grabbed her arm.

"C'mon, Lis. It's their big lick, and they killed that shit. Let them have some laughs. Shit, if they wanna swim in that money, let 'em. They ain't stupid. They know how to conduct themselves. You taught them everything they know, right?" he said in that smooth, even tone that made Kim's insides melt. "We gon' have to let them grow up now. They ain't babies no more," Keraun continued, his eyes instinctively falling on Kim. It was like he couldn't hide it sometimes. Kim blushed.

Aunt Lisa relaxed a little bit as she seemed to take what Keraun was saying into consideration. She relaxed the tensed muscles of her jaw and cracked a halfhearted smile. It wasn't lost on Kim and Donna that Aunt Lisa probably would've done anything for Keraun's smooth-talking ass. Sometimes the girls felt Keraun also knew he had Aunt Lisa's heart, but he never crossed the line. They were sure he definitely could have.

"Just stop playin' so much—and get this damn money up. I don't care what K got to say. This ain't a game," Aunt Lisa said.

"Y'all don't worry. We gon' go celebrate tonight," Keraun told the girls.

Kim laughed out loud again. She just couldn't contain the elation she felt. At that moment, surrounded by stacks of money and all the people in the world that she loved in one place, Kim decided she never wanted to be without any of them.

"Yeah, let's get real pretty and go celebrate," Kim said.

Aunt Lisa grunted a bit, but they all knew she couldn't turn down a good time. Since they were young, Aunt Lisa was known for her spunk and party spirit. She loved to dress up, kill bitches with her straight-from-the-runway looks, and have men drooling. Kim was definitely just like her. Donna preferred to be a little more low-key, but she could throw herself together when she had to.

"Y'all gon' have to give me a few hours to find a makeup artist and shit," Aunt Lisa mumbled.

They all started laughing. Keraun winked at Kim on the low.

"I'll see y'all tonight," he said. "Make sure y'all ready to slay on these hoes outchea."

"Oh, you already know," Kim said. With that, she turned and sauntered away, knowing damn well he was watching.

Kim and Donna were still riding high when they returned to their wing of the house. Kim walked over to the picture of their parents and picked it up.

"D, you think Mama and Pop would be proud of us?"

Donna looked at her sister, suddenly solemn. "Hell yeah, they would. We was young when they went missing, but I always feel them. I swear I can feel them."

Kim wiped at the new tears that sprang to her eyes. "Me too. I will never forget what happened that night they disappeared. Never."

"Neither one of us will ever forget," Donna agreed. They both stared off into the distance . . . remembering.

15 years earlier

That fateful night, loud crashing noises erupted through the house. Donna was the first to be jolted out of her sleep. A cold sweat broke out on her forehead when she heard deep, muffled voices. It sounded like men were talking in harsh murmurs right outside of her bedroom door.

More loud noises sent a shot of panic through her chest. It was as if people were ransacking the house. With her heart hammering, Donna flipped back the covers on her bed and rushed over to her little sister's bed.

"Kim," Donna whispered. "Wake up." She shook Kim's legs frantically. It took a few long minutes for Kim to finally rouse from her sleep.

"Whaa . . .?" Kim whined.

"Shh!" Donna threw her hand over her sister's mouth. "Listen," she whispered, her breath coming out in raggedy, jagged puffs.

Kim sat up, and they both listened. There were strange men laughing, but not in a happy way. As young as they were, Kim and Donna could tell it was evil laughter, something sinister.

"We have to go out there and see what's happening," Donna whispered directly in Kim's ear.

Kim nodded her head. She had always been the outspoken, courageous one anyway. She was a year and a half younger than Donna, but she was more spirited and bossy. In that moment, she was worried about her parents, whom she loved very much.

Kim and Donna crept from the bedroom and hid behind the wall at the top of the grand staircase in their house. The men were still talking, and their words were clear now.

"Make him look at me!" one of the men instructed, taking obvious delight in in what he was doing.

Kim inched over and almost fell backward when she saw her father on his knees with a gun at his temple.

"You thought you was the boss? Huh, nigga?" one of the men snarled. He hit her father with the butt of the gun, and it snapped his head back, left and right, each time they took turns hitting him. Another blow to the face caused something to crack so loud that Kim and Donna heard it all the way from where they stood. They watched in terror, seemingly rooted to the floor. Their father couldn't even open his mouth to let out a whimper, much less a scream.

"Nigga, since you so tough, I want to hear you scream, beg mercy, or I'm going to kill everyone up in this motherfucker," another one of the masked intruders gritted out, hitting their father again, this time with his leather-gloved fist.

Their father didn't budge. Kim and Donna knew how proud he was and how much he always preached about being strong. His pride wouldn't allow him to crack. It wasn't in him to let another man make him beg for his own life. Their father had had a rough life, and he had clawed his way to the top of the drug game. His reputation in the streets of Houston preceded him. He wasn't going to show weakness now.

"A'ight, nigga, if you so tough, get up and save your family, motherfucker!" one of the masked men taunted, getting close to their father's face, which was covered in blood now.

"We taking over your shit. We told you before we wanted to partner, but naw, you was too selfish, nigga," said the main instigator among the intruders. He was trying his best to provoke their father to beg for his life.

His body swayed from blow after blow, but he still didn't lift his head or give the men the satisfaction of knowing they were hurting him. That was until he heard the high-pitched screams of his daughters.

"Daddy!" Kim screamed out. "Daddy! Leave my daddy alone!" she screamed again, this time more frantically.

Her father opened his battered eyelids and fought to lift his head, turning it painfully toward the sound of his youngest daughter's voice. She darted down the stairs before Donna could grab her.

"Get off of my daddy!" Kim belted out again.

Before he knew it, Kim had thrown her arms around him. Her father's breathing became labored. Through his severely swollen eyes, her father watched as one of the men dragged Kim up from the floor by her arm.

"Well, well, now. What do we have here? A pawn? I think you gonna change your fucking mind about partnering with us now, right? If not, you might lose one today!" one of the men said evilly.

Kim squirmed and kicked and clawed at the man holding her. She was no match for him. Her father closed his eyes in anguish. He didn't want to see them do anything to his baby girl.

At that moment, Kim's heart felt like it would explode from sheer terror.

"Now, what is it going to be?" one of the men asked. The men were hard pressed to get something out of Kim and Donna's father, but it wasn't happening.

"Dom, please! Give them whatever they want . . . please," their mother, Tanzi, begged. They had dragged her back into the room. Her night clothes were ripped, and she had blood trailing down her legs. They brought her to her husband's side, bound with duct tape. Dom was unable to look at his wife. He was being emasculated right in front of his family.

"Just give them what they want!" Tanzi pleaded for help from her husband.

Even with his wife pleading and his daughter screaming, their father didn't budge. He refused to open his mouth.

"Dom!" Tanzi screamed again.

Nothing. No response.

"This muthfucka really think he the king of Houston, huh? He ain't gonna give in? We tried to be nice the first time," the leader of the attackers said.

"Mommy! Ahhhh!" Kim screamed.

"Only your man can save you now," one of the men growled as he dragged their mother by her hair.

For the first time, Kim got a good look at him. The man was so big, and his skin was so black, that he looked like a giant monster. It was a face she could never forget. He had been the only one bold enough to take off his mask.

As Kim screamed, the man hoisted their mother in the air by her throat. Kim felt vomit creep up into her throat, and her stomach clenched in horror.

"Bitch, your man is a pussy," the giant said, throwing her up against the wall. She hit it with a thud and slid down, her body going limp. She continued to scream and beg for her life as the man pounded on her. He let his fists land at will, each punch harder than the one before. Blood covered her face and the floor around her.

"Now, y'all both gonna watch me violate y'all in the worst way," the man said, spewing a wad of spit in their father's direction.

"Take off her clothes," the same man demanded, pointing toward Kim. "Daddy!" Kim screamed, her ponytails swinging as she tried to get away from her captors. The first man slapped her with so much force she hit the floor like a rag doll. She was dazed. "Aggghhh!" she cried out.

"Get off my sister." Donna's voice came out low and gruff, her small arms waving out in front of her.

"Oh, shit! This little one got a gun," one of the attackers said, seemingly amused.

Donna's heart began to pound so hard she could hear it in her ears. "I ain't playing. I will shoot."

"Little girl, put down that gun and come join your family," the lead attacker gritted.

Bang! Bang!

Donna had closed her eyes and pulled the trigger.

"Run!" her father yelled out. "Just like I taught y'all!"

Kim scrambled away from the distracted attackers, who were now tending to their boss. Donna grabbed her arm, and they bolted for the back exit of their house, just like they'd been taught. In their pajamas, the girls ran and ran and ran until they had no more steam left. They ended up behind a gas station, huffing and puffing and dying for a rest. Afraid and visibly shaken, the girls had followed their father's instructions to just get out of the house and find their way to an adult.

Donna, being older, was the protector, as usual. She had heard her mother yell, "Take care of each other!" before they bolted from the house.

"I want Mommy and Daddy," Kim whined, her bruised body throbbing.

"I'm gonna take care of you until they find us. Everything is going to be okay," Donna said, squeezing her sister closer to her.

Their legs throbbed, and Kim whined and cried the whole time between nodding off from sleep deprivation. Falling in and out of sleep, Donna saw several people pass them and stare, but no one said anything to them. It was the store owner, who'd come out to put boxes in the dumpster out back, who had finally asked the girls if they were okay.

At first, Donna lied and said they were waiting for their parents. But the store owner, noticing their bloodied pajamas and bare feet, decided to call the authorities. When the Child Protective Service workers and the police showed up, Donna and Kim had to be forcefully moved.

Kim screamed, "Leave us alone! We're waiting for Mommy and Daddy! They're coming!"

Donna played it tough and tried to kick one of the officers and run, but she was too weak to be effective. All their efforts were to no avail. They were taken away to the hospital for a medical clearance.

Donna could barely remember the ride to the hospital. She and Kim were ushered out of the police vehicle and placed in a crowded waiting area. Kim cowered under her sister's tight grip. The hospital was chaotic. There was a lot of screaming and running and throngs of white coats and scrubs.

After Donna got Kim to settle down, they sat quietly as people hustled past them. Kim's throat had gone raw from screaming. After a while, she opened her mouth, but no sound came out. Donna cradled her sister and played hard. She wanted to cry, but she had exhausted the energy necessary to produce tears.

Every now and then, someone in the waiting room would jump up and yell profanities to the triage nurse, who sat behind a thick, scratched-up piece of Plexiglass. It seemed like a lifetime before a short, fat lady with a fake black ponytail approached them.

"Hi, my name is Dorothy. I'm a case worker," the woman said softly, extending her hand toward Donna and Kim. They both ignored the woman's hand. They had been taught never to trust anyone who worked for the government—not even police.

"Listen, I know this is difficult," the woman consoled, sitting down in a hard, plastic hospital chair next to them. "But we have to figure out where your parents are, or find someone who can help you, or else we will have to take you away to foster care."

Donna's back went straight at the mention of foster care. She knew if she didn't at least speak to this lady, it would spell disaster for her and Kim. The case worker asked a series of questions, but Donna was sure to keep Kim quiet about what had actually happened. She offered up the only relative her parents had trusted over the years.

Several hours passed before Donna and Kim heard that familiar Southern drawl and loud voice, which suddenly became music to their ears.

"Where is my damn nieces at?" Aunt Lisa barked, followed by the click-clack of her signature high heels. "I know damn well y'all ain't got my babies sitting here in these dirty-ass pajamas and in this dirty-ass waiting area, where they could pick up any ol' disease! What in the hell is wrong with y'all so-called care providers?" Aunt Lisa hollered to no one in particular, switching her hips down the hospital corridor.

Kim jumped out of the seat and bounded toward Aunt Lisa.

"Oh, baby girl. I know. I know. It's going to be all right," Aunt Lisa said, softening her voice and extending her arms to accept Kim. Bending down for a hug, Aunt Lisa grabbed both girls and held onto them. "I ain't gonna let nothin' happen to y'all. Y'all safe with me. Nobody will ever hurt y'all. I would die before I let that happen," Aunt Lisa proclaimed.

The girls both felt the sincerity in her words from that day forward. Kim and Donna never saw their parents again. They never heard whether they were dead or alive. They were simply . . . missing.

Chapter 2

"I knew this shit was gon' be lit. Shit, I see a whole lotta potential licks up in here. Just like I suspected," Kim yelled in Donna's ear over the music. She had to play it off like she was interested in work and not interested in finding Keraun.

"We out for a good time. We ain't thinking about work tonight," Donna replied. She agreed with her sister: all of the Houston hot boys—wannabes and real niggas—were out. They didn't have to say anything else, nor did they have to point out the obvious. Somebody in that party was going to be their next come- up.

Kim and Donna both noticed Keraun at the same time. He was so engrossed in a conversation with a woman that included a lot of laughing and smiling that he never looked up. He never noticed Kim glaring at him across the room.

Of course, the chick that was in his face was also smiling and blushing like whatever they were sharing was making her pussy wet. Kim was seething. She immediately assumed Keraun would be treating the chick to free bottles and VIP treatment. As she continued to scan Keraun and his entourage, her insides began to sizzle. There were lots of bitches hanging around Keraun and his entourage.

"You see who I see?" Donna asked, jutting her chin in Keraun's direction.

Kim felt heat rising from her feet and spreading through her body as she watched Keraun moving like a thirsty young boy about to get his first piece.

"Who?" Kim played it off, trying her best to get her feelings under wraps. She couldn't let Donna know the truth.

"Bitch, do not act like you don't see Keraun over there. I'm hip," Donna said knowingly.

Kim, still playing it off, squinted her eyes. Her hands curled into fists on their own. She thought her heart would jump free of her chest. "I see him *now*. Now that you pointed him out. Ain't like with all these good-looking young niggas up in here I would even notice him," Kim lied.

Before she could even get her full thoughts together, Donna was on the move, pulling Kim forward.

"Wait!" Kim started, but they were already navigating their way through the sea of bodies in the club. On the way, a few dudes tried to get their attention, but Donna was focused. Dudes grabbed at Kim and Donna's hands, and some touched their arms, trying to holler at them, but Donna was so focused on Keraun it was like no one else in the club existed.

Kim knew the attention she was getting from dudes in the party meant she wasn't slacking in the looks department. Kim knew she had it going on. She was 25 years old, stood five feet, seven inches tall with curves in all the right places. She had perfect 36D breasts, a 28-inch waist, and 40-inch hips—a perfect Coke-bottle shape with a little more on the bottom than the top. Sometimes, when Aunt Lisa was mad at Kim, she would tell Kim that she was going to put her out on the ho stroll to make money with that body, instead of giving her everything like a spoiled brat.

Kim wore a black-and-white sequined Intermix romper with the back out and a pair of red Giuseppe Zanotti stilettos. She had her hair straightened, so it hung straight down her back to her butt. It was all hers, thanks to her mother, who had beautiful long hair too. Kim didn't need much makeup, because her skin was clear and glowing even without it.

Donna was also looking like a joint. She was a few shades darker than Kim, taller by a few inches, but was just as pretty in the face. Donna was a little heavier than Kim, but she carried it well. Donna wore a short haircut, which she got professionally done once a week. She wasn't as curvy as Kim, but she had enough to keep the men swooning over her.

By the time Kim and Donna made it to Keraun's table, a fine sheen of sweat danced over Kim's upper lip, and fire flashed in her eyes. She was trying her best to hold onto her composure, but the jealousy was raging inside of her like a wildfire.

Kim and Donna approached, and Keraun was still so enthralled with his company that he didn't even notice them at first.

"So, this is where you're at?" Kim yelled over the music, immediately getting in Keraun's face.

He jumped and sat up straight. They had caught him slipping, which was rare. His eyes went wide, like he was staring down death.

Kim wanted to slap him in the face just seeing the way his eyes bulged out and his mouth dropped open, but she couldn't show her real feelings in front of Donna.

The smile Keraun was wearing a few minutes earlier with the bitch quickly faded off his face. "I didn't know if y'all were coming or not. The way Lisa was talkin', y'all wasn't going nowhere," Keraun said, finally gathering his composure and putting on his usual slick demeanor.

"I told you I was coming," Kim snapped.

Donna crinkled her brow. "You a'ight? It's Keraun . . . not ya man. Right?"

Noticing Kim's dilemma, Keraun stood up and pushed away from the table. The chick Keraun had been all goo-gly eyes with a few minutes earlier had her head cocked like she was about to say something. Keraun knew what he had to do. He didn't even bother saying anything else to the girl.

"Naw, he not my man. Nothing like it," Kim said snidely, never taking her eyes off Keraun. "Oh, don't leave your friend on account of me," Kim gritted.

"Yo, sis, you good?" Donna asked, looking from Kim to Keraun and back again.

"I need a drink. Then I'll be good," Kim replied, pouting.

"I'm going to get us our own bottle," Donna said. She shot Keraun a look that said they didn't need his shit.

As soon as Donna walked off, Keraun turned toward Kim. "Baby girl, this ain't even like what it seems," he said, immediately getting close enough for her to pick up his scent.

Kim quickly softened. He knew her very well. He reached down and grabbed her hand on the low.

"Naw. You short on this! Who is that bitch? You seemed real fucking comfortable in her face," Kim growled, glar-ing at the girl and her group of friends. She was just one of the many who seemed to be enjoying all the expensive liquor Keraun and his friends had laid out on their table.

"Chill, Kim. It ain't even like that. These bitches ain't with me." Keraun tried to placate her, speaking in Kim's ear.

"Come with me. Let me talk to you," he said as he held onto her and tugged her toward the club's exit. "You ain't got shit to worry about. C'mon. You ain't never got to act like that over no next bitch. You too classy for that. Your aunt taught you better than that."

"That's not what it looked like to me. And don't bring up my aunt," Kim said, her voice beginning to crack. If Aunt Lisa found out about them, it would be hell to pay.

"You know you my only one. Stop the madness," he said. "You think it's easy for me to be around you all the time and can't just hug and kiss you when I want?" he continued, laying it on thick.

Kim felt herself softening. She wanted to believe every single thing he was saying. "This is getting more and more complicated to pull off," Kim whined, on the verge of tears. Keraun was the first and only dude she had ever fallen in love with.

"It's all good," he said, grabbing her and bringing her closer to him. He led her out of the club. "C'mon, you going with me. Fuck all this rat race shit," Keraun said once they were outside. He was breathing hard in her ear, which always made her weak.

"I . . . I . . . can't just leave my sister. Plus, Aunt Lisa's supposed to be on her way," Kim huffed.

"Donna is a big girl. I'll tell my man Swift to keep her company. Tell her you had to talk to me about a lick. I need you right now." Keraun breathed his words into Kim's ear. "Obviously, I need to show you that you who I want. And only you."

Kim's insides had already turned to mush, especially her brain. Keraun, in all his older wisdom, was saying and doing all the right things to get into her head. She wasn't thinking straight at all. She believed what he said and told herself he was right, Donna was a big girl. She had probably found a nigga or a bitch to hang with. Donna went both ways in that department. Knowing her sister, Kim was sure Donna had found a nigga to buy her a $300 bottle and offer her a free blunt by now.

"You playing, baby girl. I need you," Keraun whispered hotly in Kim's ear.

She couldn't even control her own thoughts, especially when Keraun started sucking on her ear. It was her weak spot.

Before she could protest anymore, Keraun opened the back door of his Escalade and pushed her inside. Then he climbed up into the truck, slammed the door, and planted his mouth over hers.

"Oh my God," Kim moaned. It was half protest, half acquiescence. She tried in vain to push him off. "No . . . not . . ." She also tried to stay mad at him, all to no avail.

Keraun touched her gently on her breasts—another weak spot. Kim's chest rose and fell with every touch. Keraun wasn't playing. He kissed her deeply, and their tongues danced seductively. Kim's hips pulsed involuntarily. She could feel her clitoris beating as it swelled. She let out a long gasp. She wanted to feel Keraun inside of her so badly.

Aunt Lisa's face flashed in Kim's mind for a quick second. She would lose her mind if she found out. Kim also thought about Donna. She couldn't just leave her at the club. They had come together.

"We can't. I . . . I . . . have to . . . um . . . my sister is . . ." Kim panted, unable to make complete sentences.

"Don't talk, baby girl." Keraun moved from Kim's mouth and trailed his long tongue down to her titties.

She became so weak, and her body tingled all over. She was at the point of no return now. She didn't just want Keraun; she needed him. Kim gulped in a lung full of air. It was all she could to do keep from hyperventilating. She was so gone. All logical thought left her mind.

She tried to pull Keraun's head up, but he had taken in a mouthful of her left nipple. He sucked hard and let his tongue roam over the sensitive ridges of Kim's areola. She arched her back in response. Her inner thighs quaked. She was ready to beg for the dick by the time

Keraun finished his tongue massage. They were both frantically working to get Kim out of her clothes. Her hands trembled with anticipation.

"Sit up and ride it," Keraun grunted. He quickly slid Kim's romper off as she rose up.

Although the tints on his windows were police grade, at that point, Kim was so hot she didn't care if anyone watched them. She was sure with all the moving inside, the truck was rocking from the outside. The electric pulses of lust coursing through her body sent all her inhibitions out the window.

"Damn. Your ass is fine as fuck," he murmured, his hot breath on her face.

Kim felt a mixture of fear, excitement, and lust. This scandalous, forbidden love with an older man was so exciting it made her want to cum every time. It was enough to make her eyes roll up into her head like she had just taken a long pull on the fattest purple haze–filled blunt.

"I want to feel you so bad," she groaned. "I fucking need you." She fumbled around, trying to find a comfortable position. She embedded her knees into the soft leather seats and grabbed Keraun around the neck for leverage. Then, she straddled him and eased herself down onto his long, thick, throbbing dick. As soon as the meaty girth of his love muscle filled her up, she let out a satisfied squeal. She lifted herself up and lowered down slowly at first. With each repetition, Kim picked up speed, until she was riding his dick like a jockey bouncing on a racehorse.

Keraun clutched onto her plump, round ass cheeks and squeezed. That caused the sensations she was feeling inside to intensify so much she felt like her entire inside would gush out on him.

"Shit!" he grunted. He clutched onto Kim tighter, like he never wanted to let her go.

She lifted all the way up, and this time, swirled her hips as she sat down on his dick. The feeling that rippled through her was too much to take.

"Yes! Agh!" she screamed as she bounced up and down and swirled and bounced some more. Every time she went down on it, she made sure she swirled her hips and rocked a little bit. Kim needed to make Keraun a believer. She wanted to make sure it was the best sensation for him, but also to make sure his body made contact with her clitoris. At that moment, Kim didn't care what chick Keraun had in his face earlier. In that moment, she just knew he was hers.

"I love you, baby girl," Keraun groaned.

"I love you too, baby," she panted before she could even think about what she was saying. She wasn't supposed to fall in love with him. It was supposed to be a fling, something forbidden for excitement only. It got deeper for both of them, and they couldn't deny it anymore. It was real.

"Oh, shit, K! Oh, shit!" Kim bucked even harder on his dick. "Aggh!" she belted out as she convulsed with an orgasm. Kim felt her slick love juices leaking from inside of her.

It didn't take Keraun too long to follow. He filled her up. A warm sensation heated her insides.

Kim's body went limp against his. "Oh my God." She closed her eyes and inhaled the scent of his cologne mixed with his sweat. She loved his ass, which was dangerous. If only he wasn't Aunt Lisa's best friend, then he would be perfect.

That was always the problem. Keraun was way older than Kim and had known her since she was a little girl. Aunt Lisa would lose her shit if she found out about it. Kim knew Aunt Lisa would look at it kind of like an uncle and niece being together. The struggle was so real. There had been many dudes Kim's age with money that had tried to holler, but their dicks were whack, or they were corny. Keraun had the right swag, the right dick, but not the right circumstance. It was so messed up. Kim felt lost just thinking about how long she was going to have to keep sneaking around with him—for life.

After a few minutes of silence, Keraun slapped her ass and laughed. "Damn, baby girl. Yo' ass is a true rider. You just gon' fuck ya nigga right here in my truck parked in the club parking lot. Fuck anybody who wanna look, huh?" he joked.

Kim chuckled shyly. "You the one keep sleeping on me because of my age. I told you I was a ride or die bitch. Literally," she joked back.

They both busted out laughing. That didn't last long, though. She wasn't ready to let Keraun off the hook that fast. While he was digging her out, she had temporarily forgotten about the chick in the club. It hadn't taken long for it to all come flooding back to her mind.

"So, you always go out and have chicks surrounding you?" Kim asked with an attitude. She had immediately broken up the sexy mood. She didn't care. She was younger and she loved his dick, yes, but she was not stupid.

"C'mon, baby girl. You really going back to that bullshit?" Keraun sighed and rolled his eyes.

Kim climbed off him, onto the seat. She bent over and snatched up her clothes and began getting dressed with an attitude. "Hell yeah, Keraun. I'm the one sneaking around, betraying my family to be with you, but you out here flossing with other chicks, popping bottles like you don't care," Kim whined as she shrugged into the romper with so much attitude she hit her head on the ceiling of the truck.

"You act like I don't love you, though. When I can show you, I show you," Keraun came back as he folded his limp dick back into his boxers. "I gotta act like I want somebody or my dudes gonna think I'm gay. Ain't like I can claim you and shit."

His words stung. "I'm just saying, Keraun. This is hard for us both," she snapped. "The same way your friends wondering about you, my sister and my aunt wondering about me. But you don't see me out here with every nigga in my face. Why do you think that is? Out of fucking respect for you, that's why."

"Point taken, Kim," Keraun said. He always called her baby girl, his nickname for her, unless he was getting mad. "I didn't have them bitches up there. My niggas did. You really think I care about anyone but you? Huh, Kim? I ain't got to lie at my age. If I didn't love you, I wouldn't give a fuck. A nigga definitely wouldn't be around here playing I-spy, sneak and go seek, to be with yo' ass. I'm a grown-ass man. I don't have to play kiddie games. You know that. I can't even understand why you tripping like this. It's not easy for me either, but it's either that or you will be dealing with Lisa. That's what you want? Huh? Because I'm all the way good with her knowing. I ain't the one trying to look perfect in her eyes," Keraun barked, his tone serious.

Kim lowered her eyes and shook her head. She knew he was right. The last thing she wanted was to lose him, but she also didn't know how she'd deal with Aunt Lisa too. At least now, they couldn't be out front with their shit, but he could still fuck her so right. If shit got out about them, Kim would lose on all ends. Aunt Lisa wouldn't be happy, and she sure as hell wouldn't allow it. He was supposed to be a father figure to the girls, and Kim loving him wasn't going to fly. Kim was also scared to death that her aunt would kill him if she found out.

"You're right. I'm sorry. I'm just so frustrated having to hide. This can't be life," she lamented.

There were a few minutes of uncomfortable, awkward silence that settled around them. It seemed to make the air heavy, intolerable even. Kim and Keraun both shifted uncomfortably in their seats. They were both thinking about the wrath of Aunt Lisa, but also about losing each other.

"Shit, you know your aunt better than me. Say the word and we can go tell her," Keraun said, breaking the silence.

Kim snorted and shook her head, like what he'd said was the most ridiculous thing she had ever heard. He laughed. Kim shook her head and smirked.

"Yeah, right. You must want to end up dead," she said, followed by an uneasy, fake laugh.

"Nah, it won't be me that ends up dead," Keraun said, his words trailing off.

"What?" Kim said. Her eyebrows crinkled in confusion.

There was more silence. It was like Keraun and Kim were both just thinking real hard about how things would eventually turn out with them.

"If we could be together in the open, shit would just be easier. I mean, all it takes is a word. But are you ready for that?" Keraun asked. "Are you ready to be mine all of the time with the possibility of giving up your family?" He wasn't looking at Kim. He was staring off in a zone, like his mind seemed to be racing.

Kim had to move a little on the seat, so she could look at him. "What you mean?" she asked, moving her head so that she was looking him in his eyes.

"Just what I said," he replied, throwing a knowing glance in Kim's direction. "How much you willing to give up for us . . . for this?"

Kim's heart started thumping. She crinkled her eyebrows and looked at him to see if he was serious. He couldn't be seriously asking her what she thought he was asking her.

"Sometimes in life we gotta give up one thing to get another. Sometimes we gotta lose people to have the people we want," Keraun replied seriously, rubbing his beard slowly, like he was in deep thought.

"Me without my family?" Kim repeated with an eerie tone to her voice. "That would be like trying to live with no oxygen," she said. Then she turned her face away from his and stared out of the truck's windshield. Out of her peripheral vision, she could see that Keraun was also staring straight ahead.

She didn't say another word that night, and neither did Keraun. Kim had always heard that what was understood did not have to be said. Maybe she had heard wrong. They headed straight to his place. Kim knew Donna wouldn't like it at first, but she also knew Donna couldn't be mad for long. If Keraun made Kim happy, then she would be happy for her eventually.

Chapter 3

"Baby girl, I don't want you to leave me. Stay here with me just like this, laying in my arms all day and night. No cares in the world. Just me, you, and that bomb-ass weed we copped," Keraun said sweetly as he stroked Kim's hair. Their bodies were intertwined like a pretzel—her head on his chest, his arm around her, and her legs weaved between his. This was where she wanted to stay . . . forever. It was ideal, but not real.

Kim reached over and picked up her cell phone. She closed her eyes and bit her bottom lip. Her heart immediately started thumping wildly. Six missed calls from Donna and four from Aunt Lisa. They had probably already put an APB out on her. Kim sighed loudly and unhooked herself from Keraun. This was always the hard part. She hated to have to leave, but she was there on borrowed time. Kim had been there most of the night, and if she didn't show her face by noon, there was going to be a price to pay.

"I need to go. Aunt Lisa will be flipping out, and you know she just be knowing shit. She's like the world's greatest fucking detective. Lying to her never works. If she questions me, she will know about us. Neither one of us wants that. You already know how she is," Kim lamented. It was as honest as she could be. Lying and sneaking out from under her sister and Aunt Lisa had gotten to be stressful. Kim had made up so many stories to get out that sometimes even she couldn't keep them straight.

Telling Donna and Aunt Lisa about Keraun wasn't really an option. Kim knew they would think she was too young for him, and besides, Aunt Lisa was always preaching that he was their uncle. Kim had even wondered if Aunt Lisa was saying that because maybe she had had a relationship with Keraun in the past that Kim and Donna didn't know about.

Aunt Lisa didn't really want them to date anyway. It was fine for them to use their beauty to snag niggas for the setup, but she was always preaching against them getting serious too young.

"Niggas ain't shit. Always have your own shit. Live your life before you think about settling down," Aunt Lisa would say.

"This is getting old fast. After a while, I'm going to get sick of this and just tell Lisa what it is. What she gon' do?" Keraun replied.

"I get your frustration, but I can't be caught up between you and my family. Trust me, Aunt Lisa will not back down on this. You of all people know how overprotective she is with me and Donna. After our parents disappeared, Aunt Lisa is very crazy about anything happening to us. She will literally storm the streets with her gun if either one of us is gone overnight. She would probably shoot a nigga or two out here trying to find me. Telling her wouldn't end up good for me or you," Kim said in the softest voice she could find.

"Honestly, can I ask you a question?" She knew it was a sore topic for Keraun. After all, he was powerful in his own right. He was King K on the streets, and he didn't like feeling like he had to be scared of anyone, much less a woman he thought of like a sister.

"What?"

"Did you and my aunt ever have anything going on besides, you know, business?"

Keraun sat up. He moved to the edge of the bed and turned his back toward Kim. His jaw rocked as he lit the end of the blunt they had shared earlier. He was over 40 years old, and he didn't like to be told what he could and could not have, especially by a kid. This shit with her running in and out of his life was getting old, especially because Keraun was feeling her so much.

"Listen, baby girl," Keraun said, blowing out a plume of smoke at the same time. "I get what you're saying, but what I'm saying is . . . you gon' have to make a choice sooner rather than later. I ain't one to be waiting around. Shit, we just gon' do this sneak shit forever? You know how many girls out there want to be laying in that spot in my bed where you at right now? A lot. But I'm 'round here keeping the spot warm for you—when you wanna let my shit be cold," Keraun said. He was bluffing, and he knew it.

Kim had an idea that he wanted her, but there were still some doubts. She reached out and touched his back softly, running her long, stiletto-shaped nails down his spine. "You don't mean all of that. We can't live without each other, and you know it. I know it's hard. You are old enough to be my father. You really like my uncle. I'm still basically a kid. I can't even buy liquor legally. Plus . . . you know, your whole street thing and our business. Us being together, out in the open, will definitely blur the lines. Sometimes I have to fuck a nigga or two out there to make it real enough," Kim was saying.

Keraun jumped up and threw his blunt into the ashtray on the nightstand. He turned around to face her. His face was flushed, and his nostrils flared. Kim's eyes grew wide. She knew she had said too much.

He got close to her and lowered his voice into a growl. "Don't ever talk to me about you fucking the next man. I don't ever want to hear that shit. I know what you do for a living, and you know what I do, but if you ever fuck a nigga out there, you better not let me find out. You understand?"

Kim didn't like to be talked to like that, but she understood Keraun's frustration. She exhaled a long breath. She had mixed feelings about Keraun's interest in her. When they had started messing around, she thought they had an understanding. They were just a fling. It was like now, he wanted way more from her. She had fallen in love with him, without a doubt, but the thrill of the relationship being a secret and mysterious was falling apart because he was changing shit up now. He was a big-time street nigga in Houston, with all of this supposed street cred, but on the other hand, he was sweating her in a way that made him come off a little weak. He was starting to get on her nerves, even if sometimes it was nice to feel wanted like that.

"It's like this, baby girl: I ain't telling you to either choose me or choose them. I'm telling you we gotta find out how you can do both. I ain't with the fuck and run. Then I can't see you again unless it's business? Nah," he said.

Kim jumped when she heard her cell phone buzzing on the nightstand. "Fuck," she grumbled. She had definitely stayed too long. Donna could cover for her up to a point, but after a while, Aunt Lisa would be losing her shit.

"I know. That's Lisa or Donna, right?" Keraun said, disgusted.

Against her better judgment, Kim ignored her phone. She turned her sights back on Keraun. She hated the idea of him being mad at her. She was so conflicted. There was only one thing that could set things straight, and it always worked.

"K, c'mon. Let's not fight about this. We got work to do out here, and we can't let little things stop us up. I ain't going nowhere," Kim said as she climbed back on the bed.

Keraun's entire facial expression changed. He moved back onto the bed too. Kim couldn't resist his thick, long, perfect dick. Keraun had definitely taught her and then turned her out. He might've been older, but no other dude had ever fucked Kim like Keraun did. Not only did he do magic wonders with his dick, but his tongue game was on point too. Every single time she fucked him, Kim would have multiple orgasms.

"C'mere. Let me make it all better," Kim said sexily as she put her feet flat on the bed, bent her knees, and let them fall apart, exposing her warm, velvety center. She used her middle finger to massage her clit while she made her eyes dreamy and licked her lips.

Keraun shook his head. His breathing became labored. "This the shit I'm talkin' about. You say you leaving, then you do this shit and get me open," Keraun said breathlessly. His dick was standing at attention. He couldn't resist Kim's tight, young pussy either.

She cracked a devilish smile and slid her long, slender fingers inside of her slippery hot box. "I knew this would make it better," she said right before he roughly placed his mouth on top of hers and forced his tongue between her lips. Kim loved that shit. She extended her tongue into Keraun's mouth as well, and they licked and sucked on each other's tongues with rough passion.

Keraun wedged his body between Kim's legs and prepared to enter her. He was breathing hard into the soft skin of her neck. "Am I wrong for wanting you to be here with me all the time?" he panted in her ear.

"Naw. Fuck me. Fuck me forever," Kim panted back through labored breaths. "I want you to fuck the shit out of me," she said. She knew herself to be a sexual being, borderline nymphomaniac. She wanted to explore all types of sex.

Keraun laughed at her. "Baby girl, you too young to be asking for it rough," he grunted as he held onto his goods.

Kim squinted her eyes, and then out of nowhere, she slapped him in the face, inciting him.

"Aye! What the fuck?" Keraun grunted, taken aback. He leaned up over her and glared down at her.

His evil eye didn't faze Kim one bit. She wanted what she'd asked for. She slapped him again, this time harder.

"Yo! Kim, stop playing!" Keraun barked, his face folded into a scowl. He didn't care who she was; he wasn't letting no chick hit him like that, fucking or not.

"I said fuck the shit out of me! Fuck the shit out of me!" Kim growled like she was possessed.

With his chest heaving, Keraun obliged. "A'ight, you want it like that, I'ma fucking give it to you like that," he snarled.

Kim laughed at him. She knew that would incite him further. He grabbed hold of his dick, used his knees to roughly spread her legs apart, and rammed himself inside of her with the force of a bulldozer.

Sharp pains shot through Kim's midsection like lightning bolts. That was exactly what she wanted. Her pussy creamed over from the pain. That shit hurt so good.

"Ahh! Yeah! That's all you got? Fuck me, old man!" Kim screamed out.

Keraun rammed harder this time, like he was trying to send her body through the other side of the bed.

"Ah!" she screamed louder. Her pussy was throbbing, but Kim was relentless. She lifted her hips so she could accept her punishment. "That's all you got?" she teased as she pulled her knees up toward her shoulders.

Keraun worked harder. The sound of skin slapping together echoed off the walls of his bedroom.

"Oh, shit! That's what I'm talking about! Ahhh!" Kim screamed out. She was feeling it now.

"Yeah, scream!" he gritted, ramming her over and over again.

Kim dug her nails into his shoulder. Keraun bit down into his jaw from the pain. He reared his hips back and slammed into her pelvis as hard as he could. Their hip bones crashed against one another.

"Aggghh!" Kim let out an ear-shattering scream. This time, she busted her nut all over his dick.

She smiled. "You're next," she whispered.

Just as Keraun was about to continue banging into her pussy so he could get his rocks off too, a loud crash interrupted their flow. The sound of glass shattering filled the air, followed by loud voices.

"What the—" Keraun huffed, jumping up off of Kim so he could reach for his gun.

He never got the chance to grab for it. He was literally caught butt-ass naked, dick hanging, and guilty as shit.

"You motherfucker! I knew you was being a dirty bastard behind my fucking back! Get the fuck away from my niece, you piece of shit!" Aunt Lisa screamed, her .40-cal Glock waving out in front of her.

"Aunt Lisa! Wait! Oh my God! Please!" Kim screeched, frantically grabbing for the bed sheets to cover herself. "It's not his fault! I love him! I wanted to be with him! He didn't do anything wrong!"

Earlier, Lisa had tried to call Keraun, but he never picked up. Then she thought about it hard. Kim had been spending a lot of time out and about, claiming she was working a new nigga, but it never made sense. There was no new nigga that Keraun wouldn't tell Lisa about. Her gut told her to show up at Keraun's house just to see, and if she was wrong, then he would have to get over it.

"Oh my God! Please! Don't shoot him! Please! I love him!" Kim pleaded through tears. Still wrapped in a bed sheet, she was finally able to step close enough to her aunt to get between her gun and Keraun.

Donna looked on disapprovingly and disgusted. She shook her head at Kim as if Kim should've known better than this.

Aunt Lisa's chest rose and fell rapidly, and she shook all over. The girls had only ever seen her that angry one other time, and the person at the other end of her anger didn't fare so well.

"Kim, get yo' fucking ass dressed and let's go before I shoot this trifling-ass, so-called brother of mine," Aunt Lisa gritted out.

Kim could hear the hurt behind her words.

"Lis—" Keraun started.

"Don't! Don't fucking say a word to me, K!" Aunt Lisa yelled, shaking the gun like she was about to use it. "You's a nasty bastard. She's not even old enough to buy your old ass a drink! You used to take her for ice cream! You ain't got no fucking decency!" Aunt Lisa barked, sounding like she was on the verge of tears.

Kim's jaw rocked. Not only was she embarrassed, but she wanted Aunt Lisa to know she wasn't a fucking baby anymore. She was tired of her acting like she was a kid. Kim had always listened to everything Aunt Lisa taught, but it wasn't lost on her that Aunt Lisa couldn't keep a man. How the fuck could she tell her who to love and who not to love?

"Get dressed! I'm not going to fucking say it again!" Aunt Lisa yelled through her teeth.

"C'mon, Kim. Let's go. This don't have to get bad," Donna said, looking around for Kim's clothes.

"You know what? I'm not a little girl. I'm not going. I'm staying here with Keraun. If y'all can't understand love, oh well," Kim said defiantly. It was hard for her to say the words, but it was time she made it clear that she was not a kid anymore.

Keraun's eyes went wide. He knew Aunt Lisa very well. Donna shook her head as if to say "Oh, hell no." They all looked at Kim like she'd lost her mind.

"Listen, baby girl, you go with your aunt and sister. I ain't worth all this," Keraun said, standing there naked and embarrassed, with Aunt Lisa's gun still trained on him.

"Come on, Kim. Let's just go," Donna said, trying to keep the peace.

"Bitch, I'm not asking you to come. I'm telling you that's what you about to do! You ain't staying here with this snake-ass nigga. Period," Aunt Lisa spat.

"I said I'm not going. I'm in love with K, and I'm staying here. If that means y'all won't love me anymore, then it is what it is. I can love who I want to love," Kim said through tears. She immediately regretted the words when they left her mouth, but now she had no choice but to stand by them. She just wanted Aunt Lisa and her older sister, for once, to let her live her life. She understood that something terrible had happened to their parents and everyone wanted to protect her, but they had to understand that she was going to need to spread her wings.

Donna rushed over to where Kim stood trembling and crying, but steadfast in her decision. "Kim, stop playing. You know how Aunt Lisa is. We are giving you one last chance to come home. If you choose to be here, you ain't gonna be able to come home at all," Donna said, pain and fear lacing her words.

The words reached Kim as if someone had punched her in the gut. She doubled over, crying. "Why do I have to choose? I can be with him and still be family to y'all. What's so hard? K has been in our lives forever. He loves me," she pleaded.

Kim looked down at the floor. She had to put her foot down and demand respect, but it didn't change the hurt she felt for going against her Aunt Lisa—the only person who had cared for her in the past fifteen years.

Aunt Lisa shook her head. Her nostrils were opening and closing like a raging bull. "Kim, one last time. Let's go," she gritted.

"I already told you I'm in love with K, and I'm staying here," Kim replied, her words seemingly exploding around the room.

Donna's eyes filled with tears. She threw her hands up. "Come on, Aunt Lisa. Let's go. She's grown now, and sometimes we gotta let her figure her life out on her own," Donna said, disappointed.

"No! Y'all are my babies, and she is coming with us now!" Aunt Lisa screamed at her, her voice cracking like she was going to cry.

Kim covered her face with her hands and sobbed. Donna swiped angrily at her tears.

"Baby girl, just—" Keraun started to say.

BAM!

"Oh my God!" Kim screamed and jumped as the ear-shattering sound erupted in the room. "You shot him!"

"Urgh!" Keraun moaned as he fell to the floor, holding his right arm.

"Oh my God, Aunt Lisa! You shot him! You fucking shot him!" Kim hollered as she rushed to Keraun's side. "Get out! I don't want to see you right now! Get out!" Kim screamed.

"Don't come running to us when shit don't work out with this nigga," Aunt Lisa retorted. "Let's go, Donna. She gotta learn the fucking hard way."

"You fucked up," Keraun groaned. "You took this to another level, Lisa."

"Oh my God! This is all my fault!" Kim cried. She looked up in time to see Aunt Lisa and Donna walking out on her. For the first time in her life, Kim was without her sister and her aunt, the only family she knew. She could only hope she had made the right decision.

Chapter 4

Two weeks had passed since the incident with Kim and Aunt Lisa. Donna felt like she was caught in the middle, and she was missing her sister, but she was also really angry at her for abandoning her family. Donna had never thought Kim would choose a man over her and Aunt Lisa. That shit had kept her up at night ever since the incident. Donna wanted to clear her head, and there was only one place she could really do that.

Donna drove her Lexus truck to a part of town Aunt Lisa always forbid them to go to. She was still distraught over what had gone down with Kim. Donna couldn't understand her sister's logic. They had always been taught that family came first. How could Kim even choose a man over her? Donna just wanted to clear her head. She pulled up in front of the rusted gates that surrounded what used to be a beautiful mini-mansion on acres of land—her childhood home.

Donna stared out the window, already on the verge of tears. She'd been going back there in secret for years, whenever she needed to clear her mind and feel connected to her parents.

"I fucking miss y'all," Donna whispered. She shook her head at the sight of the house that had never been sold. It was a sharp reminder of the tragic story of her parents.

Donna clasped her hand over her mouth. It was all she could do to keep from screaming as she took in an eyeful of what used to be a place she associated with love and the good life. It didn't matter how many times she came back; the effect was always the same. The place she used to call home was now reduced to looking like a haunted house with brown vines snaked over the dirty red bricks, choking off the beauty that used to be the crown jewel of the neighborhood. The windows were marked with caked-on dirt and grime, and some were cracked, with sharp shards of glass sticking at the edges.

"Daddy, what happened? How did you let all of this happen?" Donna repeated the questions she always asked every time she came. She swiped roughly at her angry tears. "We can't put the pieces of our lives back together because we will never ever have answers. Who wanted to get rid of all of us? And why?"

Donna swallowed hard and shook her head from the heavy waves of emotions washing over her. She tried to keep her memories of her mother and father alive in her mind, fearful that somehow they would fade away and never come back.

Her father, Dominick Shaw, was always larger than life in her eyes. He was a true man's man, and he was proud of his daughters. Donna and Kim loved when he would take them around and show them off. They felt so important. At that time, the girls were too young to know what he did for a living. But Donna remembered the day he bought them the new house.

"My babies will never want for anything as long as I have air in my lungs," he said that day. Moving his family out of the hood to the huge house was a big deal for Dom. Tanzi had been so happy she cried.

Donna remembered how she and Kim had raced into the house and bounded up the spiral staircase to their room.

Donna swallowed hard. She wished Kim was there with her now. The memories caused an ache deep inside of her. There were good and bad memories in that house. Donna still thought about how strange it was that no one had ever found her mother's and father's bodies after the attack. It was like the police had never even opened a case. After Donna and Kim were taken to Aunt Lisa's, they never heard another word about their parents.

Aunt Lisa lived in a tiny apartment when she first got them, and then it was as if overnight, she was able to buy a big house, then an even bigger house, and then the biggest house. Donna never questioned things, but every now and then, Kim, with her big mouth, would question their parents' disappearance. Aunt Lisa never wanted to speak about it. Aunt Lisa thought talking about the tragedy was a bad omen.

Aunt Lisa could never know Donna frequented the house when she was missing her parents. She had warned Donna and Kim that it was highly dangerous. Aunt Lisa thought people might've been watching the house, but Donna thought it was ridiculous to believe the attackers would still be watching an abandoned house fifteen years later.

Aunt Lisa always acted as if the attackers might return one day. She had all types of security devices on the house they lived in now. She was also super careful about their movements.

"We are not supposed to be separated, Kim," Donna spoke out loud as if her sister could hear her. "Daddy told us we needed to always stick together, not choose a nigga over each other," Donna gritted out. White hot, bitter tears sprang to Donna's eyes, and anger flared in her belly so fiercely she could hardly breathe just thinking about all that she and Kim had been through since their parents had disappeared: the days they spent learning how to hustle together, learning how to use their beauty and smarts to get over on a nigga.

There were good situations, and there were bad ones. Once, when Kim was hustling her first dude on her own, Donna didn't feel that she was ready, and she followed her. Donna was happy she had, because somehow, the dude knew he was being set up and almost sliced her face from ear to ear.

But now, Donna was alone. She closed her eyes and inhaled. Her father's face played out on the backs of her eyelids for a few quick seconds—his gorgeously handsome face, his muscular arms, and his beautiful smile. Donna could no longer hold back another round of tears as they fell in streams down her cheeks.

"Fuck it. I'm going inside," Donna mumbled under her breath. She usually didn't go any farther than the circular driveway, but today, she needed to feel something more. She needed to see if she could find a clue.

"I know what you said, Aunt Lisa, but I have to do this . . . for me," Donna rasped, her mouth cotton-ball dry.

Donna scrambled out of the car. Her legs were moving, but she didn't feel like she had control of them. She wobbled and bobbed, which was the result of every nerve in her body being alive and either pulsing or jittering. Her heart thrummed against her chest, and she could almost hear the screams again.

Donna kicked through the piles of dead leaves and tree branches that littered the porch. She inhaled deeply and slowly turned the knob on the front door. Surprisingly, the lock clicked, and the door creaked open. As she stepped inside, the terror Donna was feeling suddenly congealed into a sizzling ball of anger, fear, resentment, and hatred for the men who attacked them that fateful night.

"If I ever find out who they are, you can rest assured they will get it," Donna said through her teeth. Her anger propelled her forward, and the cold, abandoned house no longer scared her.

Donna navigated through the expansive property like she still lived there. The walls were covered with dirt and black spots. The once pristine house was now a complete disaster. It looked like the inside of a dumpster. She rounded corners and descended steps like she had come home to stay.

Flashes of memories played out in her mind's eye like a movie. She could see her mother in her beautiful bathroom, sitting at her gold-and-glass vanity. She could see her father in his office with his partners, talking business and smiling at her when he noticed her peeking in the doorway. She could see her father chasing her and Kim through the house while they screamed and laughed and ran away from him.

When Donna finally made it up to her parents' old master suite, she had to fight her way through thick tangles of spiderwebs and dust bunnies. The room was still as expansive as she remembered. She took in a deep breath as she looked at the ransacked space. It was obvious that whomever had attacked her mother and father that night was looking for something.

Standing in the doorway for a few seconds, Donna could still picture how beautiful the room used to be. She and Kim loved being in their parents' bedroom and playing in their mother's enormous clothing- and shoe-filled closet.

Donna turned to her left, where a huge portrait of her mother and father used to hang. It was gone, just like they were. Donna felt an unbearable ache in the center of her chest. She didn't even realize how hard she was crying until she felt her shoulders quaking and her legs shaking.

Sucking in nostrils full of snot, Donna slowly walked to their closet. She pushed the doors open, and it was still there. The safe sat open, just like Donna had left it the night she'd gone into it to get the gun.

"One-forty-six . . ." Donna huffed out the combination under her breath, just like she had that night.

Donna spun in circles, looking for any clues about her parents. She opened drawers, but they had been emptied. She walked through the closet, as if after all these years, something would stick out. Suddenly, she tripped.

"Shit," she cursed. It was a loose piece of floorboard. Donna bent down and tugged at it. The first tug didn't move anything. Donna huffed and grunted and tugged again. This time, the floorboard came up into her hand. Donna had tugged so hard that when it came loose, it caused her to fall back onto her butt.

Donna looked down into the hole, bent down, and frantically used her hands to dig inside.

"Oh, shit," she mumbled. She spotted the black bag stuffed into the floor. She tugged and tugged, and another two floorboards shook loose. Donna sucked in her breath and pulled with all her might, until it came out.

"Daddy, I forgot to get this that night," she spoke out loud as if her father could hear her. "I was so scared, all I remember was the gun. I didn't remember the emergency bag." There was so much going on that night. The fear overpowered her mind and didn't allow her to remember everything her father had told her and her sister.

Donna flopped back onto the floor and pulled her knees up to her chest. She was paralyzed by the memory that invaded her mind.

16 years earlier

"I want you girls to listen to me carefully," Dom said to his daughters, his tone serious.

"Yes, Daddy," Donna and Kim replied in unison as they trailed behind him into his closet.

"You both know that sometimes the world can be a dangerous place, right? Remember I always tell y'all this," Dom said.

"Yes, Daddy," the girls answered again, their little faces crunched in confusion. They had never seen their father act so serious. He was usually the fun parent. It was their mother that was kind of strict.

"Well, I want to show you what to do if anything ever happens to me and your mother. If you girls are ever in any danger," he said.

"Okay, Daddy."

"But remember, this is our secret. You girls can't tell anyone about this."

Donna and Kim watched their hero closely as he walked over to the big safe that was embedded in the back wall of his closet.

"Come closer so y'all can see," Dom summoned.

Both girls walked to their father and looked up at him with rapt attention.

"This is how you open a safe," he said, twisting the black dial several different ways. "The combination is . . ." He whispered it in their ears. "Now, let's practice it."

Donna and Kim had to try the safe fifteen times before their father was satisfied they knew what they were doing. They had grown exhausted after a while, and Kim started to whine.

"Shh. Everything I've been teaching y'all is for your own good. I want you both to be strong girls and to be able to protect yourself just in case anything ever happens to me or your mother," their father said seriously. "Now, no crying. You all are big girls. No babies around here."

Donna nodded. He had given her this same speech many times before, but it was the first time he thought Kim was old enough to hear it.

"Now, back to this. After you open the safe, you take this out," he said, pulling out a black, hard plastic case. "This is only for real emergencies, and it's for your protection, not to be played with," he said, opening the case.

Donna's eyes went round. Kim wasn't that interested. Wide-eyed, Donna looked at the contents of the case, and then looked up at her father and back down at the case. She was very young, but she knew exactly what it was and what it was for.

"This is what you will use to protect you and your sister, okay? You hold it like this," their father said, handing Donna a .40-caliber Glock. The gun was way too big for her hands.

"You put your hands like this and grip," their father said as he wrapped his hands around Donna's and simulated the action.

Donna did exactly what her father told her to do.

"Good girl. You're such a little lady. There is one more thing I need to show you."

Donna watched him walk to the middle of the closet and then to a corner by her mother's extensive pocket-book collection.

"Right here, you pull this up," he said, forcing up one of the floor boards.

"What's in there?" Kim asked, suddenly interested again.

"You will see," their father said, moving another floor-board to show them a black bag stuffed under the floor. Both girls looked down into the hole.

"This is the money you'll need to get away and get to someplace safe. Make sure you take it when you get the gun, okay?" he said sternly. "If you don't, you will be out there in the world with nothing, and I don't work hard for that to happen to my babies."

"Yes, Daddy," Donna and Kim sang.

"Good. That's the plan. Remember, if anything bad happens, get the gun, get the money, and y'all stick together and get out of here as fast as you can. If you have to shoot the gun, do it, but make sure y'all look out for each other and always stick together . . . for life," he said, kissing both of them on their foreheads.

"This is scary, Daddy," Donna said.

"I know, but I have to make sure you know what to do. Don't worry, I will always try to be here so that you never need that gun or that money," he said, picking them both up into his arms for big hugs. "But, like I said, just in case anything bad happens to me or Mommy..."

"Nothing bad can happen to you and Mommy. I love you, Daddy," Donna said, squeezing her father as hard as she could.

"Me too!" Kim squealed.

They all laughed and hugged right there in the closet.

Donna was sobbing at the memories. She forcefully tugged on the bag until she finally pulled it through the hole. She coughed on her tears as she thought about her father and the night they got attacked. She had forgotten the money. She felt stupid now. Years and years had passed, and she hadn't remembered about it. Without bothering to brush the dust from the top of the bag, Donna unzipped it. She shook her head at the contents—another .40-caliber Glock 23 and stacks and stacks of cash. Donna didn't want to count it now, but she was sure her father would've left enough to set her and Kim up for a while.

"Thank you, Daddy. I'm sorry I let you down and forgot about this. I'm sorry I couldn't save you and Mommy," Donna whispered, hoisting the bag onto her shoulder and rushing back out of her parents' bedroom. She thought about stopping at her old bedroom, but the painful memories were just too much to bear.

Donna hurried straight to her car. Once her bag was in the trunk, she slid into the car and exhaled a deep breath.

"You're good. You got this shit," Donna pep-talked herself.

She wanted so badly to call Kim, but she was still too furious with her sister to speak to her. After all they had been through together, Donna was heartbroken when Kim chose a man over her. Donna was conflicted, because reaching out to Kim now after she'd made her choice would be going against Aunt Lisa. Right now, Aunt Lisa was the only one who was there.

Donna could only hope that Aunt Lisa would eventually understand Kim's decision. It was one thing to be defiant against Aunt Lisa, because she was so strict, but for Kim to totally dismiss her . . . Donna didn't know when and if Aunt Lisa would ever get over that shit. Donna felt stuck, because she didn't want to disrespect Aunt Lisa, but she also couldn't go against her father's wishes. They were supposed to stick together no matter what happened.

Donna swallowed hard and tried to keep her emotions at bay. She had so much going on inside of her. Chief among her concerns was how the fuck they were going to take care of themselves if Kim decided to be away from them. Suddenly, Donna felt helpless all over again, like she had that night her parents were attacked.

"Damn you, Kim! I'm not letting shit stay like this! We are a fucking family, and we are all we got," Donna said out loud, slamming her fist on her steering wheel. "You are coming the fuck home. I don't give a fuck how grown you think you are." Donna had made up her mind. Even if Aunt Lisa didn't like it, she would have to live with it.

With that, Donna pulled away from her childhood home. She didn't see that someone had been watching her the whole time.

Kim sat alone at the end of the long, glass dining room table, staring at the empty chair across from her. The full plate of shrimp, lobster, and fettucine had become cold and stiff. The house was completely silent, which gave Kim a feeling of dread. She hated being home alone, and she hadn't been this lonely in years. Kim tried to think of a time that she had been without her big sister in her entire life, and she kept coming up short. Two weeks had passed, and Kim was ready to call Donna and Aunt Lisa and beg them for forgiveness.

Kim looked at her cell phone again for the one-hundredth time in five minutes. Still no calls, not even one call from Donna, and Keraun had not bothered to reach back since he'd left the house early that morning. Kim had tried her best to be a loyal woman. She cooked, got her hair done, and bought some new lingerie, but none of that made up for the empty feeling she had inside. Now, she couldn't stop the tears from falling. How could she have been this stupid? She'd chosen Keraun over her sister and Aunt Lisa, but she hadn't thought their stalemate would last this long. Kim thought for damn sure Donna would've reached out and asked to talk by now. Donna had always been the diplomatic one.

This wasn't how she'd envisioned her life to be with Keraun. They were supposed to be inseparable. Kim expected him to be there. She expected him to become that man she'd first snuck around with, when the time spent together was never enough. Kim did not want to be the wifey at home, only allowed to come out to play when Keraun said it was okay.

Kim thought when their relationship hit the fan that Keraun would devote his time to make sure she was good, since he knew her family would leave her alone. The first couple of days, he was there, but then Keraun would leave Kim for hours alone. At first, Kim wasn't mad about it, because he explained that he had to still make his presence known in the streets to uphold his reputation. Kim understood. Then, those hours of being alone became a routine, and there was no fighting against it.

Now, the loneness only left her to think about Aunt Lisa and her sister. When she made the choice to be with Keraun, she thought it would be all good and things would smooth over with her aunt and sister. It had been two weeks now, and Kim was feeling the results of her decision in the worst way. She wanted to call her sister. Aunt Lisa couldn't control the one she loved, Kim thought. But she knew at this point it would be damn near impossible to get through to either of them. Time had solidified her choice, and in their eyes, they only saw Kim as the one who left.

Kim wiped the tears off her cheeks. She got up and tossed her plate in the trash and threw Keraun's plate across the room.

"Fucking bastard!" she screamed. "Always leaving me alone. All you wanna do is fuck and smoke. I hate you!" She picked up the bottle of red wine she had opened and took it straight to the head.

Kim jumped when her cell phone finally buzzed on the tabletop.

"Hello?" she answered anxiously. She closed her eyes in defeat when she realized it wasn't Donna or Aunt Lisa. It wasn't Keraun either.

"Why are you fucking with my man? You must like how my pussy taste, bitch! Stop with the annoying phone calls and stay the fuck away from my man, bitch!"

"What?" Kim answered, confused.

"You stupid or deaf, bitch? Did you not just hear me? Stop fucking calling my man!"

"Who the fuck is this?" Kim questioned, her entire body going cold. More tears spilled from her eyes.

"You don't need to know who I am. All you need to do is understand he wants me, not a child, so go back to your momma, kid!"

"Get the fuck off my phone, bitch! Keraun ain't your man! He's mine, and I'm the one living with the nigga!" Kim barked into the phone. She was shaking all over. She spun around three times in circles, not know whether to go left or right. Finally, she grabbed her pocketbook. She was heading to Keraun's hangout spots. And when she found him, she was going to fuck him up!

Chapter 5

Donna drove in silence after her visit to her childhood home. She felt terrible, because all she really wanted to do was call Kim. But, she also wanted Kim to feel the pain of loneliness. Donna was relishing the quiet time, though. No Aunt Lisa yelling. No Kim whining. No stress about setting up their next lick.

Donna was thinking about her future. If her sister didn't come back, what would she do? Donna realized in that moment she had made her life about protecting Kim and living for whatever Aunt Lisa wanted for them. Donna couldn't front; she was mad at Kim, but she kind of admired her balls in standing up to Aunt Lisa like she had.

Donna shook her head. She felt like she literally had the weight of the world on her shoulders, and she was feeling overwhelmed, to say the least. Donna started to turn her car around and find a hotel, but she knew Aunt Lisa would lose her mind. Donna was the loyal one. She knew she had to go home to her aunt.

"I just want to run away from all of y'all until y'all get this shit together," Donna mumbled. She dialed Aunt Lisa's number to see if she wanted her to bring anything in for her. Donna knew her aunt well, and if she had passed all of Aunt Lisa's favorite restaurants without calling, that would be a cussing out for sure.

"Why the hell you ain't answering your damn phone?" Donna grumbled out loud. She disconnected the line and called again. No answer. Donna shook her head. It was way too early for Aunt Lisa to be sleeping, and it was a weekday, so she couldn't be hanging out. Besides, Aunt Lisa would've definitely called if she was going to hang out. A scary feeling trampled through Donna's gut. She shook it off. The thought of something happening to Aunt Lisa alone made Donna bite down into her jaw.

"Stop thinking the worst all the time," she told herself. "Aunt Lisa is fine. She's the toughest lady I know." Still, Donna stepped down on the gas and sped her Lexus truck through the streets.

She had a cold, queasy feeling inside, because it wasn't like her aunt to ignore calls. Aunt Lisa always had her phone, because it was connected to all of the ways she made her money.

Donna finally pulled up to their house, and nothing looked immediately different from the outside. She pulled into the driveway behind Aunt Lisa's Cadillac truck. It was in the same spot it had been in when Donna left the house. She threw her car in park and scrambled out of it.

As Donna climbed the grand steps in front of the house, she froze. It was as if a fist of fear reached out and grabbed her by the throat. She froze when she noticed the front door to the house ajar. There was no fucking way Aunt Lisa would have the door open. Plus, she didn't answer her phone! Donna's heart pumped hard, and her legs felt weak as she moved slowly toward the door.

"What the fuck?" she whispered. Without even thinking of her own safety, she pushed the door in and slowly stepped inside. "Aunt Lisa?" Donna called out.

She moved through the foyer slowly. She could hear loud music coming from the den area.

"Aunt Lisa!" Donna hollered, more frantically this time. There was no answer. She crept farther into the house, but she didn't see anyone. She moved slowly, peeking behind her every few seconds. Suddenly, Donna's body felt cold, like she was standing barefoot on a block of ice. A knot of pain formed at the base of her skull, and her head began pounding. Something was definitely wrong.

"Aunt Lisa, where are you?" Donna yelled out, this time louder and more frantically than before. When she got to the doorway of the den, the place they conducted most of their business, Donna slowly pushed the door open. The music assailed her ears right away.

"Aunt Lisa!" Donna called out so loudly the back of her throat burned. Once she stepped all the way into the room, her legs went weak, and she almost crumpled to the floor.

"No! No!" Donna stared at her aunt's naked, bound body, slumped over on the floor, with blood spreading under her. The back of her head was blown out, and her body was curled into a fetal position. She had been stripped, bound, put on her knees, and executed with shots to the back of her head.

"Aunt Lisa! No! No!" Donna screamed again. The smell of decomposing flesh and death choked Donna and threatened to make her throw up. Donna was immediately taken back to the night her father and mother were beaten. The sharp, metallic smell of her aunt's blood reminded her of that night.

"Agggh!" Donna screeched, falling to her knees. "No! Aunt Lisa! No! Not you! Why?" Donna squealed as she took in the sight of Aunt Lisa's brain matter on the floor and walls.

"Argh!" Donna leaned over and threw up on the floor, then she quickly sprang to her feet and stumbled backward to get away from the body.

"Oh God!" Donna cried out, whirling around. Behind her were Aunt Lisa's clothes and a bunch of money with her blood splattered all over it. "Oh my God!" Donna continued to scream, her body quaking all over.

As she went to back out the door, she noticed the message on the wall written in blood: KARMA IS A BITCH. ONE BY ONE. I JUST BEGUN.

Donna involuntarily bent over at the waist and threw up again. Her mind was fuzzy, and she felt like she couldn't walk. Who knew all the things they had done well enough to know that killing Aunt Lisa would cripple them?

Donna stumbled out of the room and rushed toward the door. She had to get out of there, but her legs didn't seem to work. She didn't even know what to do next. Instinctively, she called her sister—the only person she had left in the world.

Kim's chest heaved up and down as she listened to her sister scream on the other end of the phone. Her body rocked involuntarily. She couldn't understand what Donna was telling her. What the fuck was Donna talking about? Had she said Aunt Lisa was hurt? She didn't say dead, did she? No fucking way she said dead. What did she just say? Kim's ears were ringing, and her brain felt fried, like literally, fried.

"Arrggggh!" Kim finally belted out a scream from deep inside her soul. The information had finally settled into her brain. "No!" She felt like she was going to black out. Kim had already started waging war in her mind against whomever was responsible.

In tears, Kim returned the house she used to share with Donna and Aunt Lisa. As she exited her car, the wild scene of flashing lights and police vehicles made her head spin. She was approached at the driveway by an officer with his hands out in front of him, halting her.

"Ma'am . . ."

"This is my house! My aunt . . . my sister!" Kim boomed before he could say another word. The skinny rookie officer could try her, but no one would be able to stop her from getting to her sister.

"Okay, just park and I'll walk you up," the officer said to placate her.

With shaking hands and legs, Kim parked and got out of her car. Her head pounded, and she felt like some force beyond herself was carrying her up the driveway to the house.

"Donna!" Kim screamed as soon as she saw her sister. "Oh my God!" The floodgates of emotions had opened up. Kim dashed toward her sister.

Donna whirled around as she swiped at the tears running down her face. She barreled toward Kim like she hadn't seen her in a hundred years.

"I'm so sorry! Please forgive me! Oh my God!" Kim cried out, grabbing Donna roughly into a bear hug.

Donna's heart skipped a beat, and adrenaline rushed through her body. "Promise me . . . never again! You're all I got! Promise me." Donna broke down. Her body was wracked with sobs.

"I'm so sorry for turning my back on y'all," Kim cried. "I have been so miserable living without y'all. I fucking hate myself right now."

"I can't believe what is going on right now," Donna sobbed. "She ain't deserve no shit like this."

"I know. I hate that we were separated and mad at each other when this happened. I won't even be able to speak to her anymore . . . never going to be able to say I'm sorry or set shit straight with her again. That's all I thought about on the way here. This shit is going to be fucking hell." Kim cried into Donna's shoulder.

As they embraced, Kim noticed Keraun being escorted by a police officer to where they were standing. She had been mad at him for leaving her in the house alone for so long and his recent neglect, but all of that fell away in that moment.

"K! She's dead, K!" Kim screamed, throwing herself into Keraun's chest. Keraun was still cool, wearing his regular Houston Rockets jersey, his clothes pristine, and his swagger was on one hundred. His arm had a small bandage on it, but even that blemish didn't spoil his demeanor.

Donna wasn't so welcoming. She watched him, and something about his demeanor in that moment gave her pause. Aunt Lisa was supposed to be like his sister, and granted, she had shot him in the arm over Kim, but still, Keraun didn't seem like he was one bit fazed that she was dead. Kim didn't seem to notice.

"I'm here now, baby girl. It's gonna be all right," Keraun said, rubbing Kim's back while his eyes stayed trained on Donna.

She squinted at him in response. Tears and all, she wanted him to know she didn't all the way trust his ass. Keraun saw the look Donna gave him, but he didn't react.

"They saying anything? Ask y'all any questions yet?" Keraun asked.

Kim pulled away and turned toward Donna for answers. Donna bit down into her jaw. She didn't want to speak to that nigga, but she had to play along. She didn't want him to know that in her eyes, he was a suspect already.

"They want us to come to the station and speak to them. You know . . . ask about whether or not Aunt Lisa had any enemies," Donna replied, giving Keraun a hard look when she said the word *enemies*.

Kim shook her head. "Aunt Lisa ain't had one enemy. We have to let them know that this shit was very random," Kim said with urgency.

Donna kept her mouth shut about the message written in Aunt Lisa's blood inside the house. She was too suspicious of Keraun to let him know anything. Now all she had to do was convince Kim that Keraun might not be one to trust right now. He had said some foul shit to Aunt Lisa after she shot him, and in that moment, Donna hadn't forgotten it and wasn't going to let it go. At this point, everything about him was suspicious.

Keraun's crew was waiting outside of the perimeter that the police had made around the house. He had agreed to take Donna and Kim to the police station and stick by their sides through this tragedy.

"Yo, chief, what the fuck happening?" Juice, one of Keraun's right hands, rushed over. "When you called, we ran. What's up?"

Keraun stepped away from Kim and Donna to speak to his people. Donna acted like she couldn't hear, but she was ear hustling, while Kim rambled on about missing Aunt Lisa.

"I'ma talk to y'all off site. Too many cops out this bitch. We definitely need to talk, though," Keraun said cryptically.

Just then, they all looked up at the house in time to see Aunt Lisa's body being taken out in a black bag and loaded into coroner's van.

"No!" Kim screeched again. Donna quickly grabbed her into a tight hug. Kim bucked her body and wailed as her sister held onto her and sobbed too.

"We'll talk later," Keraun whispered to Juice. He rushed over to Kim and Donna. "C'mon. Let's get out of here. We have to figure shit out," he said, helping Kim climb into his SUV.

"You a'ight?" he asked Donna, noticing the way she was glaring at him.

"You? I mean, you seem a'ight, even though your so-called sister is dead up there," Donna said, jerking her chin toward the house.

"Somebody gotta stay calm. We can't all be around here falling apart. Don't mean I ain't feeling shit," Keraun replied. "I'm not your enemy. Trust and believe that. But if we don't work together to find out who is, one of us might be in one of them black bags next," Keraun said with eerie finality.

Chapter 6

A week had passed since Aunt Lisa's murder, and Kim and Donna had been holed up at Keraun's place. Donna would've preferred to be at a hotel, but Kim wasn't having it. Keraun had been making himself scarce. He claimed to be out on the streets trying to find out who was responsible for the heinous act against Aunt Lisa.

"I don't even want to go to this service, Donna," Kim said solemnly as she fiddled with her hair, trying to figure out whether it was appropriate for a funeral to wear it up or down.

"I have to see her in a different way than I last saw her, or that will forever stay in my mind," Donna said. "I will never forget that shit as long as I live. I want to see good pictures of her and happy times."

"I'm so sorry you had to go through that by yourself. But I was thinking that I would've probably been home with her when the shit happened if I was living here. You might've come home and found me and Aunt Lisa executed," Kim replied, her voice trailing off at the scary thought.

"I thought about that. Everything for a reason. And you know where I was that day?" Donna said.

Kim stopped fiddling and turned toward her sister. They met eye to eye.

"Where?"

"I went back to our old house," Donna said like it was a forbidden sentence.

Kim's eyes went wide. "Oh my God. For real? Aunt Lisa would've had a fit if she knew that. Remember she made us promise never to go back there and never to ask her to take us. She thought it was a bad omen," Kim said, and then her words faded as if she had just figured something out.

"What?" Donna asked in response to her sister's look.

"You think you going there was the . . . you know . . . bad omen?"

"I don't believe in that shit. Me going there helped me discover what's in the trunk of my car now. And with our house still being under the eyes of the cops, we need it."

"What are you talking about?" Kim asked.

"I'm talking about all of our money. We can't get to our safe or Aunt Lisa's safe . . . our money . . . but," Donna started explaining, but she was interrupted.

"Hey, y'all ready?" Keraun stepped into the room.

Donna exhaled. She didn't know how much he had heard.

"Give us a few more minutes," Kim said.

"Nah. We should be good," Donna interjected, giving her sister a look that said, *Not now*. Donna wanted nothing to do with Keraun, even if her sister was still blinded by her love. Donna needed to remind Kim about what their father had said to them years ago, but now was not the time. She wanted Kim to be alone without Keraun around.

Kim held onto Donna's arm as they approached the front doors of the funeral home. Donna kept her head hung low to avoid all the news media dotting the path up to the funeral home doors. Aunt Lisa's death had been plastered all over the news. The homicide detectives had held several press conferences about, as they had put it, "the woman slain execution style."

Donna knew that if they still lived in the hoods of Houston, Aunt Lisa's murder wouldn't be getting so much attention. Living out in the ritzy suburbs in such a palatial estate, the neighborhood was on high alert over what had happened. Donna had asked the detectives about the cameras in the house, but whoever committed the crime had smashed them all. There was no trace or clue as to what had happened except the cryptic message that had been left on the wall. They had drilled Donna and Kim about who might want to hurt Aunt Lisa or them, but the girls said they didn't know. Honestly, given their track record of setting dudes up to be robbed for everything they had, there was no telling who could've done it.

Donna still always had it stuck in the back of her mind that one day the people who were responsible for her parents' disappearance might come back. Everyone was always saying how much Donna looked just like her mother.

Aunt Lisa's funeral was as large as her life had been. No expense was spared on her casket, flowers, and her outfit. Everything was laid out as if she were a queen. Kim and Donna noticed that some of the biggest hustlers and most prominent businessmen in Houston were in attendance. So were all of Keraun's dudes that were a part of the team that worked to pull off the licks when Donna and Kim set dudes up.

Keraun insisted on having a lot of dudes acting as security at the funeral. He had cautioned Kim and Donna about the risk of attending the big, elaborate service without enough security, fearful that whoever killed Aunt Lisa would be waiting to make their moves on them.

Even with all that he was doing for them—letting them crash at his place, making sure they had anything they needed, and the security at the funeral—Donna still wasn't one hundred percent convinced that Keraun had nothing to do with Aunt Lisa's murder. Donna had tried to keep Kim close leading up to the funeral so she could determine what Keraun was up to, but Kim didn't know much about his moves at all.

Donna, Kim, Keraun, and Juice rode together in a black Suburban to the cemetery. Keraun held the door and looked around cautiously as Kim and Donna climbed out. They both had their eyes covered in dark shades, but it wasn't hard to see how many people had followed them there to pay their last respects to Aunt Lisa.

"She was really loved," Kim rasped, looking out at the crowd.

"For real. That's why this whole shit got me suspect right now," Donna followed up.

"No need to be suspect," Keraun said flatly. "I already told you I'm working behind the scenes to find out who did this shit."

"Can y'all just stop? I been feeling the tension between y'all from day one. I'm sick of it. Sis, I know you didn't like the whole way shit went down with me and K, but he's always been family to us," Kim proclaimed all in one breath.

Donna looked over at Keraun and shot him a dirty look, but she was going to respect her sister's wishes for the sake of peace.

"Thank you. Damn. We gotta do better. It's bad enough I have regrets about not speaking to Aunt Lisa when this shit went down. Life is just too fucking short," Kim snapped, shaking her head in disgust.

"Stick close to me and the security," Keraun said, ignoring her.

Donna wanted nothing to do with him, but she had to admit that being out there in the open with all those people, not knowing who was there to do them harm, was nerve wracking.

Suddenly, an ominous feeling came over Donna. She looked behind them, facing opposite the crowd, and she saw a heavily tinted Mercedes G-Wagen slowly creeping up around the path in the cemetery, coming toward them. Donna squinted and noticed the tip of a weapon sticking out of the back window of the vehicle. A bolt of fear struck Donna like she had been hit with lightning.

"Back inside! Get back inside!" Donna shouted, grabbing her sister and pulling her back toward the Suburban.

"Agh! What the fuck!" Kim screeched.

Keraun whirled around in the direction Donna had been looking. He noticed the car too.

"Get them inside! Now!" he boomed, but he didn't follow.

The driver, one of Keraun's hired security dudes, threw the SUV into drive and stepped on the gas, causing the vehicle to lurch forward. The tires whirred into the grass.

Donna turned around in her seat and craned her neck to see if the G-Wagen was pursing them. Screams erupted everywhere. There was a loud blast. The force of it sent Keraun flying into the dirt, and several other people were knocked down. Cemetery headstones were torn from the ground and went flying into the air. The entire place erupted into massive chaos, with people running and screaming.

"Oh my God! What was that? What the fuck is happening? Where's Keraun?" Kim asked, her eyes wide, her left hand clutching her chest. Before Donna could answer Kim's question, the sound of rapid gunfire and shattering glass cut through the Suburban.

"Donna! Niggas is shooting at us! What about Keraun? We can't just leave him!" Kim shouted, ducking down in the seat. Just then, more gunshots rang out.

"We don't have a choice! Drive! Fucking drive!" Donna commanded, banging on the back of the driver's seat. She got down on the floor of the SUV and scrambled around to find her pocketbook. She started digging into her oversized purse for the Glock she'd found at her childhood home. Thank God she had brought it for protection. Initially, she had been so skeptical of Keraun that she took the gun just in case he tried some shit, but now, she was so happy she had it to try to protect them. All of this was so surreal.

"These motherfuckers are really after us!" Donna screamed, sticking her hand out the window and firing back. The driver of the G-Wagen had gotten the balls up to pull right next to the Suburban now.

"Drive faster! Faster!" Kim screamed at the driver. More deafening shots rang out. Shot after shot hit the side of the Suburban.

"We not going out like this! Fuck this!" Donna said, squeezing off more shots at the G-Wagen.

The driver swerved the Suburban all over the road, because thanks to Kim screaming and Donna shooting, his nerves were fried to hell. More shots slammed into the SUV. This time the tires screeched against the street.

"Agggh!" Kim screeched as blood splashed on her face from the front seat. "The driver is hit! He's hit! He can't drive like that! We about to die!" Kim yelled from the back seat.

Donna couldn't concentrate on that now. She was too busy keeping the driver of the G-Wagen at bay by firing shots straight for the driver-side window.

"You gonna have to flip over the seat and drive, Kim! It's our only way to make it out of this!" Donna screamed.

Kim was a wreck, but she didn't even think twice. Her will to live was stronger than her fear at that moment. She flipped over the seat and took hold of the steering wheel. Kim was breathing hard, but she was able to wedge herself onto the driver's lap and get her foot on the gas. She didn't care that she was basically sitting on a dead man's lap. It was time to either live or die. There was no time to think about the lifeless body beneath her, or the blood soaking into the back of her clothes. It was up to her to get them out of there.

"Kim, don't stop mashing the gas or we are dead. These motherfuckers want us dead," Donna said while she struggled to fend off their attackers.

Just as the words finished leaving her mouth, the G-Wagen slammed into a pole, stopping the truck at full speed.

"Pull over! Pull over! Pull the fuck over!" Donna screamed at Kim. She planned to get out and hit up whoever was breathing inside the G-Wagen.

"No! You can't get out! Are you crazy? They are still trying to get us," Kim screamed.

"They're going to be fucking sorry they every shot at us. Fuck that! They just hit up the very spot where Aunt Lisa was supposed to be at peace," Donna huffed, gun in hand as she frantically opened the Suburban door.

"Fuck! Oh my God! Donna! You can't be serious!" Kim screamed, grabbing the door handle so she could get out too.

"Stay there! If anything happens to me, pull the fuck out," Donna yelled to Kim.

"Fuck that! I'm not letting you go it alone," Kim said. She had snatched the driver's gun off his hip. She didn't know shit about shooting really, except what they'd learned from their father when they were small. Kim had watched many movies, so if she had to use that fucking gun, she would just close her damn eyes and pull the trigger.

Kim was shaking all over as she followed Donna out of the Suburban. They carefully approached the G-Wagen with guns in their hands. Kim could barely control her breathing, but her sister seemed so calm that she looked crazy to Kim.

Donna peeked into the G-Wagen, and she could see that she had hit the driver, who was slumped over the steering wheel, his eyes wide open. There was a dude in the front passenger's seat, leaned into the door with blood all over the front of his shirt. Donna couldn't see into the rest of the vehicle.

"What are we doing?" Kim whispered harshly, her teeth chattering because she was so nervous.

Donna signaled for Kim to be quiet. She walked to the other side of the G-Wagen. Just as she made her way around the back bumper, she noticed the barrel of a gun.

"Run!" Donna called out to Kim. But Donna didn't run herself. Instead, she ducked, leveled her gun, and squeezed off. There was no time for a standoff. She didn't let her mind talk her out of anything.

Donna had just polished off the last of the hit men that were after them. The scene was like something out of an old Western movie.

From her hiding spot, Kim watched Donna rush toward the Suburban. Kim couldn't help but think about Keraun. What had happened to him? She felt numb all over her body. She was sure in her heart that he was gone. Everybody at the cemetery was probably gone. Aunt Lisa's burial service had been desecrated. Kim doubled over and dry heaved at the thought.

"C'mon. Let's go," Donna huffed. She was moving like a robot. She opened the driver's side door of the Suburban and dragged their driver's body out onto the ground without hesitation.

"We just gonna leave him?" Kim asked.

"What the fuck you think?" Donna snapped. She was a different person in that moment. Again, just like when they were kids, she was in full survive-or-die mode.

Kim sighed, and her shoulders slumped with disbelief. Her sister wasn't the same person in that moment. "I mean, he did drive us away from the danger. We could at least call 911 about his body," Kim mumbled.

"We are being hunted! What the fuck about that don't you understand?" Donna boomed as they loaded back into the SUV. "We are on the fucking run from God knows who! So, if you want to end up like him and Aunt Lisa, then go ahead and call whoever you want, but right now, my focus is on getting us someplace safe and fucking alive! You want to live, don't you? Or do you want to end up like Aunt Lisa?"

"You know I want to live! That's a stupid-ass question! You acting like you don't give a fuck anymore!" Kim looked at her sister with hurt eyes.

"Don't look at me like that! There is no time to care. We only got each other now, and we have to stick together no matter what. Promise me that?" Donna asked without losing her pace in the speeding SUV.

Kim looked at her sister and realized what she said was true. They were on their own, and Kim had to stick with her sister, her only family from now on.

Chapter 7

Donna and Kim made it out of the Houston city area unharmed. Kim had rocked back and forth in an attempt to calm her nerves for the entire ride. They hadn't said much to each other after everything that happened. Donna seemed to be laser focused as she swung the beat-up Suburban into the parking lot of a Hilton Garden Inn.

Kim opened her mouth to say something, but she just closed it back. There was no need. She knew her sister wasn't in the mood to talk, much less explain anything.

Kim could not get Keraun out of her mind. She could not stop thinking about seeing him fall into the dirt when Aunt Lisa's burial service was attacked. She could not stop thinking about what was going to happen to her and Donna. Were they going to be on the run for life? Kim was all cried out.

"We have to wait for someone," Donna said robotically.

"What? Who?" Kim asked, her eyebrows crinkled.

When she saw Donna's car pull next to them, her heart throttled up in her chest. Who the fuck could be driving Donna's car, and why?

"A friend of mine," Donna said, tugging on the door handle to get out of the Suburban.

But she telling me not to think about Keraun? Kim thought. She got out too. She wanted to know what was going on. This was her life at stake as well.

"What up?" the tall, dark, handsome man asked, moving close to Donna for a hug. "What the hell happened?"

he asked, looking at Donna's bloodied forehead, wild hair, and rumpled clothes. He nodded at Kim as she approached.

"What the hell?" Kim asked with attitude. "And how did he get your car? And why is he driving it? What the fuck is going on, D?" Kim thought she recognized the dude, but she couldn't be sure.

"Calm down, Kim. This is my friend, Brice. He's helping me out," Donna said flatly. She was careful not to use his street name. She could tell that Kim didn't recognize him, and that's what she had been hoping for.

"I needed the car," Donna said flatly. She walked around to the trunk and retrieved a big black duffle back and another small travel bag.

"Wait. You had bags packed? Like you knew something was going to happen? When did you have time to call him? And just why the fuck do you trust him?" Kim shot her questions rapid-fire. She was still trying to place his face, but it just wasn't coming to her.

Black put his hand up. "Whoa, li'l sis. I'm here for a friend. I don't even know what I'm being dragged into, ya heard?" he said. "Now you got me worried I might've walked into some shit."

"Just relax," Donna told Kim. "When we settle, I'll explain it all. Right now, we need to make sure we are safe."

"If you say so," Kim relented, eyeing the man suspiciously. She still didn't understand why it was okay to have a friend of Donna's that she didn't know, but not Keraun or one of his friends. They had known Keraun since they were little girls.

"Ain't nothing to be worried about. After our aunt's murder, we just need a little time away. We wanted to go off the grid for a little bit and didn't want anyone to know where to find us," Donna explained. "Nothing big at all," she lied with ease.

Kim wondered if she thought the dude was dumb. He could clearly see they had been in some shit. Her hair was a mess, her dress was ripped, four of her nails were broken, and she had the driver's blood all over her side and back. Donna also looked like she'd been to war. She'd bumped her head and had a small gash at her hairline. Her lip was busted from where she'd bit down into it while she was firing the gun at their attackers. They definitely looked like they'd been in some shit and wanted no parts of it.

"I ain't gotta know a whole lot. You was there for me when I lost it all and when I was locked down like an animal. I never forgot that shit. So, you called; I came running," Black said, smiling.

He still had that winning smile. He was a far cry from the man he was when he was on top of the game, but that hadn't changed Donna's feelings for him.

Kim couldn't believe her ears. She thought they told each other everything, but maybe not. She certainly didn't know Donna had been friends with this dude. That made Kim wonder what other secrets her sister had kept from her over the years.

"That's what's up. Thanks for coming right away. Sorry for making you come so far out. I guess it wouldn't be getting away if I had stayed in the H, right?" Donna replied, followed by a nervous chuckle. "Still, you ain't mention it to nobody, right?" she clarified.

"Naw. You know me. I don't talk to niggas like that. I stays to myself. Ain't nobody hold me down like you did when I was down and out. I respected that shit. I respected that you asked for privacy. Ain't nothing to worry about. A nigga like me can be trusted . . . fully," Black reassured her.

The tension in Donna's body eased a little bit, and she smiled. She believed him. "Good. I knew you would come through. As we know, there are not a lot of people you can trust in the world," Donna said.

She couldn't help it. She kept looking around and over Black's shoulder suspiciously. Checking her surroundings, like her father had once taught her, had become second nature. She didn't give a shit if she looked crazy and paranoid. She also didn't care that it was making Kim nervous. This was about their survival now. They had no one left to protect or take care of them.

"So, all I need you to do is use one of your IDs to get the hotel room," Donna told Black.

Kim still wore an expression like she didn't trust his ass, but desperate times call for desperate measures. And she couldn't front. On the surface, it was a good idea. Besides that, they had no choice. This dude was their last resort.

"You ain't said nothing but a word, sis," Black said.

He looked like he was struggling to believe Donna's simple need-a-break story. Donna could tell by the skeptical creases in his forehead and the glint of doubt in his eyes. Donna didn't care if he believed her or not, so long as he did the favor for her. Donna knew that chances were she was never going to see Black again after that day. She had to use him for what he was worth right then.

"I just need it for a few nights. Just get the room for two nights. That way it won't look like we staying too long, nothing suspicious. We will figure out the rest as we go. Here's some cash," Donna said, turning away so she could dig into the duffle bag. She turned back and handed Black some bills. He looked down at the cash and back up at Donna. She knew exactly why, too.

"Just tell them you don't want to give your credit card, and you want to pay all the days in cash. They will try to force you to leave a credit card for incidentals, but just tell them you'll pay in all cash. You can leave a two-hundred-dollar cash deposit for the incidentals. Don't let them tell you no shit and try to force you about no fucking credit card either. We all know cash is king. Even if you need to slide the front desk bitch a few bucks of her own," Donna instructed firmly.

Black nodded his agreement. He took the cash from Donna and licked his lips. He was too smooth for Kim's liking. Something about him was real snaky. He was a fine-ass specimen of a man with deep, chocolate skin and the nicest waves Kim had ever seen. Still, he didn't seem trustworthy for shit, and he still felt too eerily familiar for Kim's liking.

Kim and Donna watched as he casually bopped into the hotel. Kim had a raised eyebrow, but looking at her sister's calm demeanor told her that Donna didn't get a bad feeling about her handsome friend. Donna seemed overconfident she had made the right choice in getting him to help them. Aunt Lisa had taught them never to trust anyone that easily.

When Black was gone from their sight, Donna turned toward Kim. "This is the bag Daddy left in the house. Remember he wanted to show us how to shoot and stuff?" she said to Kim.

"I don't remember a lot from back then unless something triggers a memory. I guess I put all of that out of my mind," Kim admitted. "It's just so weird that you went back there and then all of this crazy stuff started happening."

Donna sighed. "I don't think that had anything to do with it. It wasn't my first time going back there alone. For all we know, one of these licks we hit might be coming back on us. I definitely don't think it has anything to do with me going to the house," Donna replied, annoyed by what her sister was insinuating.

"I'm just saying. All of this feels like we are living in a nightmare. Like someone put some voodoo shit on us or something."

Donna agreed. "It is fucking nuts what's going on."

They were going to have to get to the bottom of who was after them and get them first.

"Donna, where you know this dude from?"

"Why you worried 'bout all that? We alive and breathing, right? And the only shit you should be worried 'bout is staying that way!" Donna huffed, looking at her phone again.

"Aunt Lisa always told us to never trust anyone so easily, but you just put this nigga on to where we at, and who knows? If the price is right, he might open his mouth!" Kim still couldn't place his face, but she knew there was a reason her gut was doing uppercuts to alert her.

"Kim, you should just relax and let me handle it. No need to worry about it. I got us."

"When did you have the time to call him anyway?"

"Just so you can leave this matter alone, I will tell you when I had the time! Before the funeral, I texted him, because I didn't trust 'your man' to protect us. We was on the fucking news! Our fucking faces. Do you think whoever killed Aunt Lisa would just leave shit alone? Whoever did that shit wanted us too! Do you get that?"

"So you knew what was going to happen!" Kim looked at Donna in disappointment.

"No, I didn't, but I wasn't taking any fucking chances. Don't you get that?" Donna was boiling at this point and wanted to smack the reality into her sister. She looked at her phone again, feeling kind of anxious. She didn't want to have egg on her face if Black wasn't to be trusted.

"Do you know who killed Aunt Lisa?" Kim looked to Donna for a clear answer.

"No, but it could have been any one of those licks we set up."

"I don't know what to say. Yeah, I guess you're right, but can you think of which one?"

"Come on, Kim. Be serious. Do you remember each lick we did since we started?" Donna rolled her eyes.

"No, but shit, we gotta figure this shit out, 'cause if we don't, we just might get got unexpectedly. We need to know who we can trust."

It took Black longer than Donna expected to get the room, which made her uneasy. She had probably checked her cell phone clock a hundred times in the twenty minutes Black had been inside. Finally, Donna saw him exiting the lobby of the hotel and walking toward the cars. Black had a sexy grin on his face. That put Donna at ease. Her shoulders slumped with relief, and she grinned back. She remembered the days when his smile had made her whole world shine bright.

"You good. Just like you said, that bitch inside tried to force me give her a credit card. She even said she would have to call a manager for approval. But I did what you said. Money in her hand worked like a motherfuckin' charm. She ain't say shit else. Probably more money than she makes in a whole week. She was real nice after that. Wanted to give me her number and all that. Good thing you got some cash to spare," Black relayed, amused. "I got them keys and a number," he followed up.

"Keys? Did you get more than one?" Donna asked. She was on alert, and nothing was getting past her ears.

"Oh, nah. I only got one key, just like you asked."

"Oh, okay," Donna replied. She scolded herself silently for being so damn suspicious of everyone. "Ahh, for real you're a lifesaver." Donna smiled, taking the key from him. "You always got a hundred favors with me. As soon as I get back to the H, I'll hit you up. I definitely owe you a night out or something good," Donna lied.

Kim twisted her lips and looked down at her broken nails like she kind of figured her sister was lying, but she played it off anyway.

"C'mon. It's nothing. I don't need shit as a payback. I'm glad to help out. Anything else I can do to help you, just holler at me," Black replied.

Donna reached out and gave him a hug. "That's what's up. I appreciate you," she said honestly. The friendly hug was awkward. They both tensed up.

"Pshh, I appreciate you too. I respect your come up and your drive out here in the streets. I didn't forget you how you turned me down after I got back home, though," Black said, laughing at his last sentence.

Donna's eyebrows flew up into arches. She was taken aback by what he'd said. She felt a little guilty. He was right. They'd met and fell for each other. He was supposed to be a lick, but Donna had fallen for him. Donna fucked around with Black on the low. When he got knocked, she visited him when she could get away, and she kept his books on point. He always professed his love for her. She couldn't front; she had always loved him. But once he got home, it changed. There was too much time and water under the bridge at that point. She saw him off and on at first, but shit got too serious too fast. She wanted to keep him in hiding because she wanted to protect him from herself. She hadn't bothered to explain all of that to him. Donna certainly hadn't expected him to mention it at that moment. She let out a nervous laugh.

"You know I always got love for you. Real love," Donna assured him. "Thank you so much again for coming through for me." Donna just wanted to get away from him now. There was suddenly uncomfortable energy between them.

"Nah, no problem. I forgive you. I think," he said, followed by a fake laugh. "You went from being mine to putting me in the brother zone, right? It's all understood. We all need a helping hand every now and then. I really didn't mind coming through for you. In fact, it was my pleasure . . . really," Black continued. "Anyway, y'all stay up. I won't tell anyone I saw you." Black smiled. He moved in and gave Donna a quick hug.

"Thanks again," Donna said.

"I'll see you soon. Let me know if you need me," Black called out over his shoulder.

There was something about his parting smile that seemed sinister to Kim. But then again, she didn't trust him from the minute he arrived. The nigga still seem suspect to me," she said. "And where the fuck do I know him from?"

Donna sucked her teeth and grumbled something. "Just c'mon so we can talk about our next moves," she said.

As she started walking ahead and Kim lagged behind her, Donna turned slightly, noticing out of the corner of her eye that Kim was using her cell phone. Donna immediately felt flushed with stomach-churning nerves.

"What the hell are you doing? Who the fuck you calling?" Donna snapped, stopping in her tracks.

Kim ignored her and twisted her face into a scowl.

"I'm serious! Who the hell are you calling? We can't let anyone know where we are, and we can't afford for anyone to track our phones!" Donna growled. "Get the fuck off the phone!"

Kim rolled her eyes. She was tired of Donna bossing her around. It was okay for her to have some random nigga get them a room, but she wasn't supposed to be trying to find out about Keraun's safety?

Frustrated, Kim waved her hand in front of Donna's face. "I don't care what you say. I need to try to find out about Keraun," Kim gritted. "What the fuck is your problem?"

"Kim, do you understand that we can't trust anyone right now? We don't know who is after us. We don't know if Keraun even had anything to do with Aunt Lisa's murder," Donna blurted.

There, she had said it. She had been trying to hold it in, but the floodgates of truth had opened up now. From day one, she suspected that Keraun might have had something to do with Aunt Lisa's murder. Donna remembered the evil look on his face when Aunt Lisa had shot him in the heat of the moment.

"You can't be fucking serious, Donna. He was like a brother to her," Kim growled, her voice cracking with emotion.

"Yeah, and he still betrayed her by fucking you. Did you forget 'bout that?" Donna spat. It was a low blow, and she knew it.

In a kneejerk reaction, Kim slapped Donna in the face. Donna's hand flew up to her cheek, and she went to hit her sister back, but tires squealing in the lot gave them pause.

They both whirled around, eyes wide. It was just some teenagers playing in their car, but it was a wakeup call. It could've been someone running up on Kim and Donna again.

"We need to get inside. Now!" Donna grumbled, her entire body hot with a mixture of fear and anger.

With that, they headed inside the hotel. Donna's mind was racing. She didn't know why it was so hard for her sister to understand that everyone they loved was now dead or missing. Kim hadn't seen the gruesome truth about what happened to Aunt Lisa. Donna thought maybe if her sister had witnessed what she had seen, she would be more careful and serious about their safety. Donna was disgusted with Kim. She couldn't hide it either.

Once they were inside their room, Kim flopped down on one of the beds and put her face in her hands. The sobs came quick and furious.

Donna softened a bit. She hated to see her sister cry. "I'm sorry," Donna said with feeling. "I just need to protect you. Kim, I would fucking die if something happened to you right now. We are literally all we have left. We have to be smart right now about our moves."

"I'm sorry too," Kim said.

"I don't want to be hard on you, but this is a stressful time for both of us. I just want us to get out of this alive, Kim. I'm not saying that Keraun is a bad guy, but we just don't know who to trust right now. Once the dust is settled, you can reconnect with him. Shit, you can run off into the sunset with him if that's what you want for your life, but for now, no phone calls. And most importantly, no fighting and beef between us. Deal?" Donna said.

Kim nodded her head. "Deal," she replied in a soft voice.

"Good. Now, let's get some rest. We have to sort out our next move," Donna said and started taking off her clothes.

They both knew that meant no more discussing it. What was understood didn't need to be said. It was clear to them both that all they had was each other.

Donna was grateful for a safe place for her and Kim to lay low, but she still wasn't at ease. As soon as she made up with Kim, she quickly went about closing up the blinds before she went to take a shower. She wasn't taking any chances. Whoever was after them wouldn't be interested in talking, explaining, or negotiating. Their pursuers had sent a clear message that it was going to execution.

Kim was obviously exhausted. She threw herself stomach first in the center of one of the beds and sprawled out with her arms and legs splayed wide.

When Donna came out of the shower, she saw Kim laid out, and she finally felt like she could do the same. All the dirt and blood was down the drain, and now Donna and Kim could rest up without the worry of someone showing up to put two bullets in their heads.

"Oh my God. I didn't even realize how tired I was. I guess adrenaline will do that to you," Kim said. "This bed feels like heaven. Like the best bed I've ever been in, and we know there is nothing better than your own bed."

Donna laughed. She walked over to the other bed and flopped down on her back. "I see what you mean. This definitely feels like heaven," she said.

"Yeah, your little dude really came through," Kim said.

"Shit yeah. He was definitely a lifesaver," Donna said. She closed her eyes, exhausted. Kim was talking, but after a few minutes, Donna couldn't hear her. Sleep overcame her so fast she didn't even know what hit her. But then . . . something actually hit her.

The force of the blow to her head instantly and violently yanked Donna out of her sleep. She opened her mouth to scream, but the pain kept her from making the sound. Her eyes and mouth popped open in shock. She felt like a ten-ton metal weight had been dropped on her face.

She gulped for breath as the sleep finally started to clear from her brain. Donna realized then that her mouth and nose were covered. The panic set in, and she finally came all the way alive.

Donna moaned, kicking feverishly and trying to move her head and fight off the attack. Her throat burned with a scream, but she couldn't get it out. She couldn't see either. All she could think about was her sister. Donna could smell and taste the leather from the glove that was suffocating her. She moved and thrashed like she'd been hit with a live wire of electricity. She kicked wildly, but another blow, this time to her chest, abruptly stopped her movements. Donna felt vomit leap up from her stomach into her throat. She tried to gag, but she couldn't do anything. This was it. They had found her and were going to kill her. The next vicious punch to her stomach deflated her. The blow had landed with so much force that it made a small bit of urine escape Donna's bladder.

"Keep the fuck still or your sister is dead, right now, right here," the assailant hissed.

Tears drained from the sides of Donna's eyes, but still, she went stock still at the mention of Kim. Donna's head pounded.

They had found them. But how? How had someone gotten into the room without kicking in the door? There had been no warning signs before the attackers were standing over Donna and Kim.

Donna felt herself being hoisted up and moved. Instinctively, she extended her arms, trying to find something to hold on to. Her fighting was no match for her attacker. The next thing she felt was her legs hitting the floor with a thud. The force sent shockwaves of pain up her legs and reverberated through her spine. She was being dragged, and the carpet burned her skin. Donna tried to twist her body, but again, she was no match.

Finally, she got a glimpse of Kim. Donna tried to scream, but the sound was just muffled moans. Donna saw that Kim had a black material bag over her head. Seeing that spurned Donna into action again. She started to fight with every ounce of power she had left. She reared her arm back and drove her elbow into the attacker's balls.

"Agh!" he wheezed and bent over slightly. But that still didn't make him let go of his tight grip on Donna. "Bitch!" he growled, clamping down with even more force. "Now your ass done made me mad."

Donna groaned under his black-gloved hand, twisting her body and fighting. What did she have to lose? She felt like she was about to die anyway. She raised her hands and began punching and clawing at her attacker, but the gloves kept her from being able to dig her nails into his skin. Donna was breathing hard and going wild, bucking her body with the ferocity of a caged animal trying to get away. The constant movement made it increasingly difficult for the dude to keep such a tight grasp on her.

"I swear, bitch, I'll spill your fucking brains right now," he hissed. "Where the fuck is the money?"

Donna was no match for his power, but she kept fighting. She tried to drop her body weight down in order to loosen his grip on her. That little stunt just made the angry assailant tighten his grip on her face even harder. Donna's neck felt like it would snap from her shoulders. The pain rocking through her neck, back, and spine made her legs go limp. Finally, she had fought herself out. She was exhausted. Donna realized that with one false move, the man could've snapped her neck and ended her life instantly.

"You're a dead bitch," the man snarled in her ear. "But not before I make you watch me murder her." He forcefully turned Donna toward Kim, who was being held by another masked man.

Donna gulped and swallowed the large lump that had formed in her throat. At this point, she didn't care if they killed her, but she had to do whatever it took to save Kim. She stopped fighting.

"Yeah. That-a-girl. You learn quick," the evil bastard said as Donna finally went still. "Now, where is the money? And don't lie, because if you do, she's dead."

There was something eerily familiar about the assailant's voice. So familiar that the sound of it made her body go cold, like someone had pumped ice water into her veins. Donna's mind was so jumbled with thoughts of death that she couldn't immediately place the voice, but she knew she had heard it before.

There was a commotion to her left. She stretched her eyes to see what was happening. Donna groaned her protest as she watched the other guy throw Kim over his shoulder like a big sack of potatoes. Kim's head dangled precariously over his back. She looked like a lifeless rag doll.

"Mmm! Mmm!" Donna groaned louder, writhing in protest once again as the guy hauled Kim's limp body through the door.

No! No! Donna screamed in her head. They couldn't separate her from her sister! She really wouldn't keep still after that. She kicked her legs and twisted her body like a fish out of water. She didn't care anymore if they killed her. Donna needed to know where they were taking her sister.

Her tears came fast and in streams so long they ran over her attacker's gloves. Donna kept writhing, trying to flail and kick. Her mind was going black. She felt like she was about to leave the earth. She couldn't understand why Kim hadn't been screaming, kicking, or fighting. Was she already dead? Why else would a spitfire like Kim have been quiet in a time like this?

Donna shook her head up and down, letting her attacker know she would give them the money.

"Good. Point to where it is," he hissed, his breath hot on her face. Donna pointed to Kim's bed. The attacker signaled another dude, who rushed toward the bed. He looked under it, and then looked under Donna's side.

"She's lying. Kill these bitches," he said.

Donna shook her head. She moved her hands, signaling him to lift up the mattress. He did, and he found the cash in stacks.

"Good girl. You knew better," the dude holding her said viciously.

The other dude that had taken the money came and stood in front of Donna, and she watched in horror as he sprayed something on a cloth and got closer to her. The one holding her removed his hand for a second.

"Help! Help me!" she screamed. Her screams were short-lived before the one with the cloth forced it over her nose and mouth. Because she was screaming at the time, Donna had her mouth wide open, and whatever chemical was on the cloth went straight to the back of her throat and into her system.

Donna's nostrils burned, and she started coughing and wheezing. She couldn't catch her breath. Her eyes, nose, and throat burned like she'd swallowed a fire sword. Donna felt herself getting woozy. She was moving one minute, and the next it was difficult to even keep control of her body parts. Her ears started ringing. She wanted badly to lift her hands to cover them, but she couldn't get her hands to cooperate with her brain.

Suddenly, the room began to spin. Donna could hear voices, but they sounded like they were coming through a tunnel. She could sense movement around her. Donna fought to keep her eyes open, but she was losing. Darkness started closing in on her. She felt her chest heaving up and down. Donna opened her mouth and managed a scream, but it was short-lived, and so was her consciousness. Suddenly, blackness engulfed her.

Chapter 8

Donna sucked in her breath and jumped up as she came back into consciousness. Her arms flailed so wildly she banged her knuckles on the nightstand next to the hotel bed. Her chest heaved up and down like she had been running a race. Sweat covered her face and had her hair plastered to the sides of her face. Donna had goose bumps all over her body. Her mind was fuzzy, and she had a massive headache.

"Ah." She winced as she moved her head around frantically, looking for Kim. "Ki . . . Kim," Donna rasped. Her throat felt like it had been torched.

Donna sat up, and the room immediately began spinning. She touched her face roughly to make sure she was okay. The last thing she remembered was having a gun in her face and being held down. She looked over and noticed that Kim was curled in a fetal position on the other bed and nothing was covering her head like before.

Head spinning and legs weak, Donna didn't care. She rushed over and grabbed Kim by the shoulders to shake her. "Kim! Kim!" Donna called out, shaking her sister frantically. "Kim, you have to wake up. Please. Wake up," she called out in a panic.

Kim groaned, and her eyes fluttered open slightly. Donna's shoulders fell with relief.

"Kim, I'm right here. Please, sit up. Come on," Donna pleaded, urging Kim to move so that she would know she was all right.

"What happened?" Kim said, her voice gruff from being knocked out.

"Oh my God!" Donna cried, pulling Kim into a tight embrace. "You're okay. You're okay." Donna didn't want to let her sister go. She was so scared that something had happened to her.

Donna quickly moved Kim's face from side to side to check for bruises. She looked at her body, and there was nothing.

"Did someone hurt you?" Kim asked, pulling away so she could look at Donna.

"They robbed us and knocked us out. I think they used chloroform," Donna said, using the tips of her fingers to rub her aching temples.

"But who . . . how?" Kim mumbled, her mind obviously still clouded.

Donna's mind was cloudy too from the chloroform, and it just wasn't making any sense to her. The last thing she remembered was getting out of the shower and lying on the bed.

"Donna . . . what happened? Your face is bruised. What do you remember?" Kim tried to get up but fell right back down. Her head was pounding, and her throat was dry as the desert. "I need some water."

Donna stood to her feet but still felt dizzy. With careful steps, she walked over to the desk where the mini fridge was positioned. She opened it with a sense of urgency. Donna took out two bottles of water and walked back over to the bed, handing one to her sister. Kim almost finished it in one gulp.

"Slow down, Kim. Take it easy," Donna said as she sipped from her bottle.

"It feels like I haven't drank water in days, though," Kim answered.

"Just take it easy, Kim."

After a few minutes, Kim felt better and got up. She walked over to the mini fridge and pulled out another bottle of water. She stood and drank the entire bottle then looked to Donna. "Donna, who did this to us?"

Donna sighed. "It had to be . . ." Her voice trailed off. It was too painful to even speak the name. Not him. Not this. "There was only one person who knew where we were, Kim."

"I fucking knew it! That slimy motherfucker! Didn't I tell you not to trust him? Fuck, didn't you remember Aunt Lisa saying never to trust anyone that easily?" Kim was angry now.

"I know that the door was locked, but somehow they must've gotten a key at the front desk."

"It wasn't them who got the key, remember? It was your dude. He slipped and told us, too. Nah, you was too caught up. Now what?"

"They took most of the money Daddy left, so now we have to go into plan B," Donna explained. Donna had hidden a few stacks of cash in the bathroom in the vent before she took her shower. Aunt Lisa had always told them never to keep all their cash in one spot.

"Plan B?" Kim asked.

"Yeah. Aunt Lisa's emergency plan. Remember?" Donna said.

"But that means . . ." Kim started. Kim didn't like plan B. It was only to be used in an emergency. If plan B was to happen, that only meant one thing. Kim would have to be apart from Donna until shit was over with. There would be little to no contact with her sister for who knows how long. Kim's insides were churning, and she hated to admit Donna was right. She went to sit next to Donna on the bed.

"Can we do anything else? I just don't think it's a good idea for us to separate right now."

"We have to do what we have to do, sis. It's obvious the way we're doing things isn't working. You remember everything she taught us about the stash spots and being on the low so we're not detected? Now's the time we have to put that plan to work," Donna explained, still rubbing her temples like even she was skeptical of the plan.

"But that means separating from you?" Kim asked, her voice cracking with emotion in response to the reality of what Donna was saying.

Still a little dazed, Donna reached out and hugged Kim. "When we finally gather our thoughts enough to attempt to get out of this hotel, we'll have to be smart about this. Change clothes. Hair color. And the biggest of all, going solo until we can meet up at the agreed spot. I am never going to be away from you forever. We will meet back up, but we'll have to navigate separately to get there safely," Donna said.

Kim's face immediately folded. She started biting her nails down to the quick. Even with her head a little fuzzy, she jumped up and started moving around with nervous energy.

"This ain't about money, Donna. I just have a feeling this is about revenge," Kim said, gnawing on her thumbnail.

Donna let out a long sigh. She really didn't want to go over this again. They had already speculated a thousand times about who was after them and why. Donna and Kim had become slick and cunning women in the streets of Houston. Unless a nigga had a sixth sense, they could be set up by Donna and Kim. No one was off limits, but they preferred to target the most notorious drug dealers that had risen to multimillion dollar status. If Kim and Donna wanted it, they would find a way to take it. Now, they had to worry that one of those big-time dealers was out for revenge. As they went through the list of possible enemies, Donna had blamed a hundred people around Houston. It had all been for nothing, though. Donna and Kim still had no damn clue if Aunt Lisa's murder was related to their profession, jealousy, or even to their past.

"All of our most important family members are gone. Like, this is some kind of sick game God is playing with us," Kim said. "You still don't think this has anything to do with you going back to the house? That it's some kind of message?"

"Kim . . . please. We already been over this. Somebody definitely is sending us a message, but that shit doesn't have anything to do with me going to the house. We don't know what Aunt Lisa had gotten into. We don't know who was mad at her. We don't know which one of these niggas we been setting up in the streets found us," Donna replied, annoyed.

"But who? I mean, who would go as far as just killing her to send a message? Shit, just rob us, take your shit back. I know what you keep saying, Donna, but there is more to this. You would think this shit is way more personal than we know," Kim said.

For a moment, Kim and Donna both stopped speaking and moving. They were quiet. The thoughts had hit them both like punches to the gut. There were so many possibilities it seemed impossible to narrow it down.

"I'll be back. Keep this door locked up. Don't open it for nobody," Donna said, breaking the silence as she stood up and started toward the door.

"What? Where the fuck are you going without me?" Kim got to her feet and raced to the door before Donna could get to it. "You're not going out there by yourself. You're not leaving me here like this. Niggas busting up in here. Obviously, somebody is watching us. Hell no. You are not leaving without me," Kim proclaimed, blocking the door with her body. Kim wasn't having it.

Donna sighed loudly and shook her head. She knew her sister was dead serious. Kim was not letting her out of that door.

"C'mon, sis. I'm good. This is my role in our lives. Daddy left me to protect you. I take the risk so you don't have to," Donna said. "Plus, the one thing they didn't get when they robbed us was this." She lifted her shirt a little so Kim could see the handle of a gun. "I have to go find us some disguises. I can't sit here all day like we don't have to get the hell out of here. I promise I'll be right back when I'm finished. You know me. I never break promises to you, Kim. Ain't nothing going to happen to me, because I know I have to live for you," Donna said confidently.

Kim could tell Donna was a little nervous about leaving too. Tears instantly sprang to Kim's eyes. With everything that was going on, she couldn't even imagine something happening to her sister.

"Please, D. Just stay right now. Tomorrow we can leave together and split up and run. It's just one more day. We just have to survive one more day. Don't go out there. If anything happened to you, I'd die," Kim cried. Her entire body quaked with sobs.

Donna walked over and pulled her sister into a tight embrace. "Shh. I love you, sis" she whispered. That just seemed to make Kim sob even more. "Listen, sis. I'm good. I just need to make this quick run. We have to be on our shit right now. I'll be back before you know it. I'm not going to let anything happen to me and risk something happening to you. Never. I told you when we was little girls that I won't ever let shit happen to you, and I meant it," Donna said.

Kim wasn't having it. Her sister's words were no consolation. But Kim also knew when Donna was determined, there would be no stopping her.

"Don't leave this room, Kim. And don't call nobody—including Keraun. I love you," Donna said sternly and softly at the same time.

Kim shook her head from side to side. If something happened to Donna, at least Kim knew that her sister loved her. She was too emotional to speak in that moment, but her sister couldn't possibly know how much Kim loved her.

"A'ight. Just lock up. I'll be back as fast as I can," Donna said.

Kim's stomach churned with terror as Donna unlocked the door and pulled it open. Kim stood behind Donna, waiting to lock it once she left, but Donna stopped right before she got all the way out the doorway.

"What? What is it?" Kim asked.

Donna didn't say anything. Instead, she just bent down and picked up a box that had been left at their door.

"What is that?" Kim asked, craning her neck to see around Donna so she could get a better look. "Who is the package for? Is it addressed to one of us?" she pressed.

Donna carried the box back into the hotel room. "Lock the door back," she whispered in a low, gruff, demanding tone.

"Are you going to open that? What if it's a bomb?" Kim asked, her eyes wide. "What do you think it is? I don't know if you should. . . ." Kim rambled. She was making Donna nervous with her frantic questions.

"Be quiet!" Donna snapped. "Just be quiet." Donna threw her hands up in front of her. Donna's nerves were frazzled enough without Kim's pressing questions.

Donna was falling apart inside, but she was playing it cool. She didn't say a word. She calmly walked to the side of the room, set the box on the little table, and used her car key to cut the tape away from the cardboard. Kim rushed over. Donna's heart galloped in her chest.

Kim bounced on her legs like she had to pee. The entire room was eerily quiet. There wasn't even the sound of breathing, which meant they were both holding their breath.

"What is it?" Kim asked again. She couldn't help herself. The anticipation was killing her.

Donna shot Kim an evil look. They both turned their attention back to the strange package. All they could see was wadded newspaper at first. Donna slowly removed the top layer of newspaper.

"Aggh!" Donna shrieked, stumbling backward from the box and its contents so fast she almost fell. She had her hand over her mouth and nose.

"Oh my God!" Kim screamed. "Oh my God! Get it out of here!" She had seen what was inside.

Donna's mouth hung open. She wanted to scream, but no sound would come. She knew that she was in shock, because even the pungent smell of death couldn't help her move her feet, which seemed like they'd suddenly grown roots into the floor. Donna could not take her eyes off the human heart in the box. Dried blood covered it, and loose arteries and jagged flesh around it told Donna and Kim that it had been violently cut out of a body. Someone had sent them a human heart in a box like it was a gift. Kim's legs finally gave out, and she collapsed to the floor. Donna leaned over and threw up.

After a few minutes, they both hollered. All they could think about was that they were next.

Chapter 9

"We have two places to go before we get out. All we have to do is split up, make it to each place, and keep our eyes and ears open for anything and anyone suspicious . . . and then we can meet back up at the safe place," Donna said seriously, trying to keep herself together after being shaken up. She whipped her car out of the hotel parking lot. After the box, they had abandoned the plan of Donna going out alone to try to get hair dye and disguises.

"I don't think I can do this," Kim said, her voice cracking.

"So, just like we discussed, I'll drop you to the bus, so you can make it to the first place. We just have to make sure nobody is following us and nothing goes down," Donna continued like Kim hadn't said anything at all.

"Did you hear what I said?" Kim asked, this time more frantically.

Donna saw that Kim's hands were trembling and her legs were moving up and down involuntarily. Donna reached down and grabbed one of her sister's hands and gave it a reassuring squeeze.

"Kim, it's all good. We been through worse. We're going to get the money and get out before anything else happens," Donna said calmly. She inhaled deeply and exhaled. Even she didn't believe her own words. Things were happening back to back, and Donna was starting to feel like none of it was a coincidence or bad luck.

"This is just too much," Kim said, her bottom lip trembling. "Let me just call Keraun and ask him for help."

"Have I ever let anything happen to you since Mama and Papa disappeared?" Donna asked.

Kim shook her head.

"Well, I'm damn sure not going to now. I always have your back and front. Remember that."

Donna knew she had to keep Kim grounded, but she was having a hard time even convincing herself that they'd make it out of all of this alive.

"I believe you," Kim said.

"Good. You should. I have a pretty good track record since we were little," Donna replied with a dry chuckle.

Secretly, she was saying a silent prayer that she didn't let her sister down like she'd obviously let Aunt Lisa down. Things were crazy. Donna was just hoping that she could keep them both alive.

Kim had hot tears welling up in her eyes as Donna spoke to her. They'd gone back and forth about this so much that Donna had lost her patience.

"But, I don't—"

"Kim!" Donna snapped, cutting her words short. "We have to do this right now. Snap out of it. You don't have Aunt Lisa to tell you what to do. You have to take care of yourself. The life we knew is over and will never be the same again. You have to get that through your head. You can't think of yourself as just a pretty face anymore. You have to be smart and on your toes." Donna almost wanted to take Kim by the shoulders and just shake her. She hated to be so blunt with Kim when she knew her sister was nervous and stressed, but it was the only way to drive home her point. They were both on edge, but acting weak wasn't going to do them any good.

Seeing her sister this emotional was not easy for Donna. She remembered the night they escaped their home as little girls, how hard Kim had cried. Donna turned her face away and bit down into her jaw, trying to keep it together. Her mother, father, Aunt Lisa, and Kim were all she had in the world, and now Kim was the only one left. This was the hardest thing ever.

For Kim, the thought of being away from Donna was sending surfing sized waves of nausea through her gut. She thought Donna would just take her wherever she went. Kim exhaled. She wanted to stay positive, but it was hard.

"The truth is, you may never see me again," Kim said solemnly.

Donna shook her head left to right. "Don't say that," she whispered breathlessly. "Don't fucking say that, Kim!" She was growing angry. "I don't want to hear you speaking like that. Do you understand?" Donna gritted.

"It's true. I can't see how this will work. I can't even think straight. I don't even remember this plan, and you just told it to me ten minutes ago. Somebody sent us a fucking human heart in a fucking box, yet no one was supposed to know where we were at! Your dude turned on us. We are already fucking dead in my eyes!" Kim yelled. She was losing it.

"Don't fucking talk like this, Kim! Stop!" Donna growled, her chest heaving up and down fiercely. It took all the strength she could muster, as Donna watched Kim literally falling apart in front of her eyes.

"Repeat after me," Donna said. "We will be together before we know it."

Kim bit down into her lip.

"Say it!" Donna boomed. "We will be together before we know it!"

Kim inhaled a deep breath, wiped her eyes roughly, and then shook her head in the affirmative. "Okay. We will be to . . . together . . . before we, we . . . know it," Kim managed.

Donna gave Kim an assured smile and said, "Perfect."

Donna looked in the rearview mirror and saw a parked SUV with some suspects just sitting there. It looked like they were staring at her car. Donna continued to drive.

"Donna, what are you doing? You just passed the station."

Donna didn't answer her. She just kept looking in the rearview mirror.

Kim's nerves reappeared. Her hands started to shake again, and she was looking back to see what Donna was seeing.

"Kim, just relax. I'm just making sure no one is following us, okay?" Donna's nerves were on edge, and she had to stay calm so that Kim wouldn't lose her shit again. Donna reached for Kim's shaking hand and squeezed it, trying to reassure her that everything was all good.

"Okay, Donna. You sure you ain't only just saying that?"

"No. Trust me."

Donna looked into her rearview and didn't see the SUV anymore. She still didn't want to take any chances, so she drove around the bus station three times before finally pulling in.

Donna looked at her cell phone and realized that she only had ten minutes left until her sister's bus arrived. She parked the car in the lot and headed into the station with Kim. There were a lot of people moving around, and she could see Kim was anxious.

Donna stood in front of Kim and held her hand. "Now, listen. I don't care what happens. Not under any circumstance do you go back to the H. Not now or ever . . . even for me," Donna emphasized, staring deeply into Kim's eyes, ensuring she got the message loud and clear. Kim nodded her agreement.

"Fucking promise me, Kim," Donna said firmly.

"I won't go back to the H. I promise," Kim said weakly, with her fingers and toes secretly crossed like she always did as a kid when she was lying. The truth was, if Kim found out that Keraun was still alive, and if Donna ever needed her back in the H, she would go back and do anything necessary for them. Kim knew she couldn't really swear not to return there.

"Just be smart," Donna said, giving her a half-hearted smile. "I know I don't have to tell you that. You always were the prettiest and smartest one in the family," Donna joked.

Kim returned a tiny smile. It was the first time in days they'd been able to have a light moment amid all the stress and heavy gloom they had been under in the days since Aunt Lisa's death.

The announcement came over the loudspeaker that the bus for Louisiana had just arrived and it was time to board. Suddenly, the bus station seemed vast and scary. Kim looked around, and every face there made her jumpy.

"This is not goodbye. It's see you later. You hear me?" Donna said, noticing the scared look on Kim's face.

"Yup, just see you later, not goodbye," Kim replied, feeling herself choking up. She knew Donna was right about what she'd said earlier: she couldn't afford to get weak now.

"Sis, I promise that I will do whatever it takes to see you again, just like we planned. Promise," Donna said, grabbing her sister in a bear hug. Kim couldn't control the flow of tears now.

"Take this and use it wisely," Donna said, stuffing the last rubber-banded stack of cash that the robbers didn't get into Kim's hand. "Keep your eyes and ears open, just like Aunt Lisa taught us."

"Just like Aunt Lisa taught us," Kim repeated with a weak smile, salty tears on her lips.

"C'mon. We can't be out here crying and shit," Donna said.

With that, they rushed toward the bus.

Donna watched Kim through the window as she walked toward the back of the bus. She covered her eyes in dark shades and watched the bus pull off.

Kim watched Donna turn and rush away. As the bus inched slowly toward the bus depot exit gates, Kim got to her feet.

"Driver! Driver!" Kim jumped up, screaming. "Wait! Don't leave! I need to get off!"

The bus driver slammed on the brakes.

"I need to get off," Kim repeated as she ran down the aisle of the bus toward the exit.

Once she was off the bus, Kim ran back into the bus station. She pulled out her cell phone. She had already betrayed everything Donna had told her to do, but Kim didn't care. She knew that if she had told Donna she wasn't going to Louisiana, Donna would've flipped out, worrying about her. There was no reasoning with Donna after the mess they had gone through. Besides, Kim knew Donna wasn't feeling right since she knew it was her dude that set them up.

"I will see you at our last spot, but I have to find Keraun, and I have to figure out who is after us before they get you," Kim mumbled as if she were speaking to her sister. "I'm a big girl, and I got this. I will make sure I see you again for sure, but when I do, all these niggas would have been taken care of," Kim promised out loud as if Donna could somehow hear her promise.

Chapter 10

Kim frantically dialed the number of the person she had been thinking about the whole time. Kim's heart jolted when Keraun's smooth voice filtered through the phone. She could picture his handsome face as her eyes closed involuntarily.

"Keraun?" Kim breathed. The relief that he was alive washed over her like a warm ocean wave. Thank God he wasn't dead!

"Kim?" Keraun replied, excitement evident in his tone. "Yo! Baby girl, where the fuck are you? Where is your sister?"

"W—wait, Keraun. I'm so happy to hear your voice," Kim rushed her words out, and tears immediately sprang to her eyes. "Yes, your baby girl is alive and well," she cried. "I need your help. There are people after us, probably the same people who murdered Aunt Lisa," she managed to say all in one breath.

"You ain't got to tell me. They fucking killed my man Dre at the cemetery. I just barely escaped. What the fuck is going on? Who can it be?" Keraun replied, sounding like he was just as distraught as Kim. "This shit is all they're talking about in the streets," he continued.

"I know. Me and Donna split up. It's what we learned a long time ago from Aunt Lisa," Kim blabbed.

"Let me come get you," Keraun said without hesitation. "I can't think about you out there alone. I can protect you, baby girl."

Kim's heart melted. This was what she needed. The love she had for Keraun trumped everything Donna had warned her about. Kim wrung her hands together, closed her eyes, and slumped down onto the toilet seat of the bus station's bathroom. She couldn't wait to see Keraun.

"You're the love of my life," she whispered right before the tears of joy and relief slid down her face.

"You know what it is. You know I got big love for you," Keraun said sincerely. "Just tell me where you at, and it's taken care of."

An hour and a half later, Kim was climbing into a tricked-out SUV with huge rims. The truck was so flashy, Kim immediately shook her head.

"Aye, shawty. You my man's baby girl?" young dude with every single one of his teeth covered in gold and diamonds said as he opened the back door for Kim.

"I . . . I guess," Kim answered tentatively, looking at the over-the-top rap video extra who was apparently now her safe ride to Keraun.

"A'ight then," the young dude said, rubbing his chin as he gave her a once over, closed the door, and rushed around to the driver's seat.

Kim's mind raced with thoughts of where she was going and what she was doing. On the one hand, she worried about what Donna would say, but on the other hand, she needed to see Keraun. She couldn't wait to touch his smooth skin and feel him embrace her.

Kim said nothing during the ride. Even if she wanted to, the loud trap music the young dude blared in his truck wouldn't have allowed for good conversation. The ride seemed to be taking forever, too. Kim thought about Donna and what she would say if she knew Kim had veered off their plan. If she found out, she would be so mad, but she had to know that Kim was not ready to be alone.

Kim sat in silence, blocking out the music, and thought hard about who could be after them. She was coming up with too many individuals. There was a long list of dudes they had set up, and that wasn't even including their aunt's list or who she fucked over.

The thought of seeing Keraun quickly changed her worried mind. She couldn't wait to get him into her arms, to feel his strong arms around her, smell his scent into her nostrils, and most of all, feel his hardness inside of her. Kim was getting wet just thinking about it.

After what seemed like an eternity, the gaudy SUV turned onto a long, dusty one-lane road with nothing surrounding it but trees and bushes. She'd never seen this spot before. Where was she going? Did she make a mistake? There was a small brick structure in the distance. Kim's heart started pounding. The thought of seeing, touching, and kissing Keraun gave her chills. The SUV finally stopped. Kim craned her neck to see out the window.

"A'right shawty, this you," the country-ass young dude said, his accent thicker than the weeds growing around the place.

Kim looked out and squinted her eyes. *What in the hell? What would Keraun be doing out here?*

"This looks like some backwoods shit. You sure Keraun is here?" Kim asked the dude, confused. Her eyebrows were dipped low on her forehead and her lips were twisted.

"Aye, shawty, I just did what I was told. Big K gotchu from here on out. Said just tell you go inside and wait on him," he said like he didn't have a care in the world about her concerns.

Kim sighed loudly. She was in no position to be picky. She guessed being way out on some remote country property was better than being a sitting duck in Houston, waiting to get murdered.

"So, you gotta load out now," the young dude said impatiently.

Kim slowly exited the SUV. She was hesitant about just being left out in the boondocks with nothing or no one for what seemed like miles. It looked like no one lived here. The weeds and grass were damn near as tall as Kim's waist. There was something about this that didn't sit right with her, but she was all in now.

Kim walked slowly to the door of the short brick building. It wasn't quite a warehouse, but it wasn't country-looking enough to be a farmhouse or silo either. She turned the knob and pushed the door in, stepping into vast darkness. Up until now, she thought she'd made the right decision by going against her sister for a second time, but now she was second-guessing herself. The door slamming behind her caused her to almost jump out of her skin.

"What the fuck, Keraun?" she whispered, her throat so dry she felt like she couldn't even swallow her own spit. Kim fumbled with her cell phone so she could use the flashlight feature.

"Baby girl?" That familiar voice was like the sweetest music to Kim's ears. She squinted and struggled to see past the bright light on her phone.

"Keraun? Oh my God, Keraun, is that you?" Kim called out. "Keraun!" she called out.

"Yes! Baby girl! It's me . . . in the flesh!" Keraun yelled in response, grabbing her hands and pulling her toward him.

Kim had never been so glad to see any man in her entire life, but seeing the man she loved was more of an added bonus. She threw her arms around his neck and squeezed him like she never wanted to let him go.

"I'm happy to see you too, baby girl," Keraun mumbled, barely able to breathe because she was squeezing him so tight.

He led her through the dark building to a room. "You're all sweaty. You was sweating bullets, huh?" he joked.

"Don't joke about bullets," Kim snapped. "I been through a bunch of shit, and I'm exhausted. I need more than a damn shower."

"I hear you," Keraun conceded. "I'm sorry I couldn't protect you. Everything happened so fast, and I couldn't even move to react."

"I know. I'm sorry too. I couldn't get in touch with you because Donna was bugging. She just didn't know who to trust, and she sure wasn't gonna let me contact you, even if it was just see if you made it out alive," Kim said.

"You still look good to me," Keraun commented, examining Kim up and down carefully.

"I look like shit. Stop lying to me," Kim grumbled, knowing he was just trying to make her feel better.

She noticed that Keraun looked relaxed, like he hadn't been stressing one bit. It made her a bit uneasy, but she ignored the feeling. She needed him right then.

"Stop that," Keraun replied. "You always look beautiful to me, and that ain't no bullshit. I missed you so much."

Kim blushed. "Thank you, K. It's just been so much. I have no idea who is after us, but whoever it is, they're not giving up."

"Shh, I'm here now. Ain't nothing going to happen to you," Keraun said, pulling her into his chest for a hug.

Kim blushed again. This time she couldn't help the big smile that involuntarily spread across her face. Keraun, in all of his older wisdom, had a way with words that went straight for her heart. She would never stop loving him.

After sneaking around with Keraun, Kim had been put in the position to choose him over her sister and aunt, and she had painfully chosen him. However, up until the day Aunt Lisa was killed, Kim still had suspicions that Keraun was messing with other chicks. Now she shook off the thoughts as best she could. She needed him, and it was not the time to bring up old matters.

"C'mon. We getting out of here. I'm going to take you to my new spot. My on-the-low spot," Keraun said, leading her by the hand to his awaiting Suburban. His words sounded like music to Kim's ears. She had been craving a real shower and a warm and comfortable bed. She wondered where her sister was. Donna told her to get rid of the cell phone and meet her at their agreed spot in two days. Kim had to figure things out before then, or else she would have some serious explaining to do.

Keraun pulled his heavily tinted, all-black Suburban into the garage of a quaint single-family home in a quiet, upper-middle-class neighborhood outside of Houston. The outside of the home looked subtle, with a fresh-cut lawn out front, white picket fence, and half brick front, just like any other cookie-cutter house on a suburban block.

Kim looked around curiously, because the place they'd lived in was a chic condo in downtown Houston. Knowing Keraun like she did, she didn't think this house was somewhere he would rest his head. Kim was curious about why he had brought her there. It looked more like a house for a family with two kids and a dog. Kim's alert radar immediately went into overdrive. Did he have another chick, or even a child? He was not the one to even think about living out here like he was a family man. Keraun always stayed in the streets. Or was he here pretending? Kim's mind raced, but she didn't say anything right away.

"Home sweet home," Keraun announced cheerfully as the garage door went up and he pulled the vehicle inside and closed the garage door behind them.

Kim didn't say anything, but the look on her face probably spoke volumes.

"Don't look so happy to be here, baby girl," Keraun commented sarcastically.

Kim climbed out of the SUV and followed Keraun through a door that led from the garage into a mudroom.

"You like it?" Keraun asked her.

"Um, it just don't seem like a place you would stay," Kim said with a hint of attitude.

"Oh, that's why you look all crazy in the face. Nah, we gotta change shit up. This is just one of the chill spots I kept for when I want to escape from the madness. Not even my boys know about it. So, I figured since we both need to be on the low, this would be the perfect place until we can figure out our next move. Obviously, somebody out there got smoke for us both," Keraun said as he walked ahead of Kim, leading her into the kitchen.

Kim quickly eased her mind and let the attitude slip away. She spun around and took in the inside of the house. The plain outside would've never given her a clue that the inside was so well decorated. The kitchen boasted beautiful, shiny gray hardwood floors, white diamond-speckled marble countertops, oversized white cabinets, a huge stainless steel stove, and a stainless steel refrigerator that was built into the wall. Top-of-the-line art deco light fixtures dangled over the expansive island, which had a deep stainless steel sink. The windows had custom-made window treatments that had diamond accents bordering the tops.

"This is hot, Keraun, but I know you ain't match all of this together," Kim said skeptically. It was definitely a place she could see herself calling home in the future.

"Stop it, baby girl. You need to relax off all that suspicious shit. You know me or naw?" he said, smiling.

Kim's face flushed. Maybe she was being overly suspicious. She hadn't felt so jealous about him before.

"I bought the crib already furnished. I needed a place, and they needed a buyer. The perfect marriage," Keraun said. He was so damn smart, and that had always turned Kim on.

"C'mon. Let me show you the rest . . . and the most important part," he said, grabbing Kim's hand and pulling her toward the steps that led up to the bedrooms. Kim felt sparks as soon as her skin touched his again.

Once they got upstairs, Keraun led Kim to the master bedroom. "I can see us living here happily ever after," he said, stepping inside.

Kim immediately feel in love with the décor in the master bedroom. It was both masculine and classy, with slate gray walls, plush off-white carpet, silver-and-glass accents, and a huge California king bed with a gray-and-silver grand, high-back, tufted headboard.

"I couldn't wait to see you. I missed you, baby girl. For real, I'm an old dude, and I ain't never really feel like this about nobody else," Keraun said. "I did something special for you." He nodded toward the bed, where he had all types of goodies laid out. There was a thick, plush chenille bathrobe, Carol's Daughter shampoo, conditioner, bath gel, and facial products. There was also a gift box of her favorite Gucci perfume and a beautiful lace Savage X Fenty loungewear set.

"Oh my God! You're so sweet, Keraun," Kim gushed on the verge of tears.

"You know how I do," Keraun said sexily. "Go ahead and get cleaned up. I have some business to take care of. Make yourself at home, and I'll be back after a while."

"You're going to leave me alone? After we've been apart so long?" Kim whined.

"I promise it'll only be a few. I'll be back before you know it." He kissed her on her forehead affectionately, which completely melted her heart.

Alone in the house, Kim finished her much-needed self-pampering session, wrapped herself in the comfortable robe, climbed up on the huge bed, and flicked on the T.V. She was immediately glued to the screen when she saw pictures of her, Aunt Lisa, and Donna flashing across the screen with the huge headline flashing SISTERS WANTED FOR MURDER OF THEIR AUNT.

Kim slapped her hand over her mouth, and her body went completely cold. "What? What the fuck—"

"The manhunt for two deadly sisters is still underway in Houston, Texas and the surrounding states. Police officials report that the sisters, Kim and Donna Shaw, are fugitives wanted in the murder of their aunt and caretaker, Lisa Braxton. It is believed the sisters' motive might have been tied to a four-million-dollar life insurance policy their aunt recently purchased. Police say the deadly pair of sisters also staged a shootout at Braxton's burial to throw police off their trail. Several people were injured, and one killed during the melee at the cemetery. If you have any information regarding the whereabouts of these deadly women, please contact the police immediately. Police warn that the sisters should be considered armed and extremely dangerous," the reporter said.

"Oh my God! No fucking way!" Kim screamed, jumping up from the bed. "How the fuck could they accuse us of Aunt Lisa's murder?"

Kim fell back on the bed, her legs suddenly too weak to stand. As she lay there for a few minutes, staring up at the ceiling, her head spun, and her ears rang. She was suddenly overcome with emotion. Between being on the run for her life and the shock of seeing herself and Donna on the news as most-wanted fugitives, her body finally conked out. Mental exhaustion was too much. She lay there for a few minutes, contemplating her next move.

She knew using her cell phone to call Donna was out. In fact, she needed to get rid of the cell phone in case they were tracking her with it. She grabbed the phone and raced down the steps toward the front door, but before she could get there, it swung open. Kim jumped so hard she felt like she would have a heart attack. Her entire body was drenched in sweat.

"Hey, you," Kim huffed out in labored breaths when she realized it was Keraun. She was breathing like she had just run a race, and her chest rose and fell rapidly. Her nerves were on edge, and her mind raced with whether she should say anything to Keraun. Did he even know? She knew how he felt about bringing heat to his door. Kim was now confused, because if she told him, he might be the one to give her up, or if he already knew, then he might just be holding her up until the police showed up. Kim was regretting her decision for the second time.

"What's up, baby girl?" Keraun asked, his face folded in confusion.

"Oh my God. Nothing. You just scared me," she said, whirling around like she was about to go into the kitchen. She clutched the front of the robe in an attempt to hide the material that was vibrating from her heart beating so fast. She felt like she was suffocating.

"You sure? You look scared to death right now. What's up?" Keraun asked, moving in on her.

Kim stepped away from him. "What do you know, Keraun? Tell me the fucking truth!" Kim screamed at him. She had to know what was going on since her face was plastered all over the news.

"Whoa, whoa!" Keraun threw his hands up defensively.

Kim blinked rapidly and moved restlessly on her legs. Suddenly she didn't trust him.

"What the hell got into you? You bugging," he said. "I'm not your enemy, baby girl. Remember? Now, what changed?" he continued, keeping his voice level once he noticed her rocking jaw.

Kim breathed out a long breath. She relaxed a little bit and backhanded the sweat off her head. She swallowed hard and tried to calm her entire body from shaking all over. "Did you know they were pinning Aunt Lisa's murder on us? I . . . I just don't know who to trust anymore. How could they think we would do anything to her . . . and like that?" Kim covered her face as tears fell from her eyes.

"Shhh." Keraun grabbed her. "How would I know that? I'm here with you. Now, tell me what you heard."

"I was watching the news, and they . . . they said we . . . me and Donna—" Kim stopped, breaking down.

"What? What did they say?" Keraun comforted, stroking her hair.

"They said we murdered Aunt Lisa for insurance money." Kim sobbed. "We would never do that! Why would we? She was all we had left in the world! They said she had a four-million-dollar insurance policy . . . but we didn't know that shit! We paid for her funeral with cash she had stashed. What the fuck is going on?" Kim cried, her body quaking with sobs.

"This is crazy. They must have their facts wrong," Keraun said softly, kissing the top of Kim's head. "We will get to the bottom of it."

"I don't think I should be here," Kim started.

"Look. I'm here for you right now. You can't be out there." Keraun said, moving in to kiss her.

"But—"

"But nothing," Keraun whispered, forcefully placing his mouth on top of hers.

Although she was a bit taken aback by his bold action, Kim didn't protest. She gave in, just like she had so many times before. She was weak for Keraun, and he knew it just like she knew it. This wasn't the time for this, but the hot feeling of wanting that was growing between her legs let her know that what was happening was meant to be.

Keraun's hands moved sensually over her body, sending stabs of heat all over her skin. She was burning up inside and out. She could feel herself getting wet in more than one place.

Kim finally opened her mouth and accepted Keraun's tongue inside. Their tongues danced over each other with sensual twists and turns that sent heated sparks all over her body. Her mind was suddenly and strangely at ease, even at a time like this. Thoughts of Aunt Lisa being dead and Donna being in trouble and on the run as a fugitive, and Keraun maybe being an enemy, suddenly fell away from her consciousness. In that moment, Kim only thought about herself and her own satisfaction.

Keraun moved his mouth from hers and trailed his tongue down her neck with the expertise of a pro. With him, it was always like the first time. He always made her feel like he was taking his time with her. Keraun treated her body like a piece of rare gold or a priceless gem.

This should've been the last thing on her mind, but Kim was all in now. It hadn't taken much . . . his simple touch had done it. She let out a low grunt and a mouth full of air with each of his movements. Her body felt like it was engulfed in heat. She was overwhelmed by the feelings that were taking over her body as Keraun trailed his tongue lower and lower. Kim's legs tingled and trembled, her stomach quivered, and her pussy throbbed like a heartbeat.

"I missed you," Keraun whispered just before he took in a mouthful of her nipple.

"I missed you too," Kim panted, twisting her hips toward him, egging him on, because she couldn't control the throbbing between her legs.

As soon as the breathless words left her mouth, Keraun moved his tongue to her stomach. He licked gently past her belly button and then around the triangle of her love mound. It was a little unkempt down there because she had been away from home and not able to really keep things up, but Keraun didn't seem to mind that at all. He still took his time, tasting every inch of her like he never wanted to stop. Kim let out a soft moan, and at the same time, he used his hands to gently part her legs.

She winced in ecstasy, letting her legs fall apart to accommodate him. She put her hand on the top of his head to make sure he didn't change his mind. Kim wanted to feel him now. All her problems had dissipated in that moment.

Keraun gently drove his pointer finger into her tight hole, while vigorously flicking his tongue over her swollen clitoris.

"Uhhhh," Kim moaned.

"Shit. I missed this sweet stuff," Keraun huffed, feeling how tight she was. "Damn, I love this shit," he mumbled as he moved his long tongue from her clitoris to her dripping wet hot box. Her juices dripped from inside of her creamy center and down to her ass cheeks.

"You are so fucking wet, baby girl. You're driving me wild."

Keraun licked every drop like he needed her juices to survive. Kim moaned and groaned like crazy. She thrust her hips forward, dying for him to continue. Her legs trembled with anticipation.

Suddenly, Keraun stopped. He was no longer touching her or kissing her body. Nothing. Kim's eyes popped open, scared that something was wrong to make him stop. She relaxed once she knew that he'd stopped to get fully undressed. With pure love in her eyes, she watched him take off his boxers and wife beater. She stared at his exposed muscular chest and legs and his long tool that had always driven her wild. Kim licked her lips. She was hungry for him, gone in the head when it came to Keraun. In that moment, nothing else mattered.

Keraun climbed back onto the bed and used his knees to gently part her legs. Kim closed her eyes, gripped the sides of the sheets, and braced herself.

"Ohhh," she cried out in pleasure as he slowly entered her with his thick, throbbing dick. "Oh my God!" she screamed out as the pain, mixed with pleasure, spread through her body.

"Damn, baby girl, you are tight as shit," he wolfed. He was going wild himself. He moved his hips with vigor, but not so much to hurt her. Because of the grip of her tight walls, he was ready to cum within minutes.

Keraun pulled his dick out before he exploded. "Whoa, this shit is so good a nigga 'bout to bust."

Kim giggled. It was always what he said about her. From day one, he'd been telling her how good she was.

"Ride it," he whispered. "I fucking missed you. I want to see you."

Kim did as she was told and flipped over so that she was on top. Keraun lay flat, and she mounted him. Placing her hands on his chest for leverage, she slowly eased herself down on his rod.

"Fuck!" she belted out as waves of pain shot through her abdomen and ass. "I missed this shit so much," Kim huffed, easing up some. It felt like his dick was touching her stomach from the inside. She began moving up and down like she was riding a pony.

Keraun grunted and panted in pure ecstasy. His legs began to shake as he tried to keep himself from busting a nut. It was all to no avail. He growled, grabbing Kim around her waist and pulling her down so that her chest was flat against his.

"Shit! This pussy is so fucking good!" he wheezed as the last of his fluids squeezed out of him. He moved so he could drive his tongue deep into her mouth and they kissed passionately as they both finished up their intense orgasms.

After a few minutes, both of their bodies, slick with sweat, collapsed against one another. Silence fell around them, and only the rapid beat of their hearts could be heard.

It was all that Kim had hoped for and more, but the pain of knowing it would all be short-lived was putting a damper on her mood. She knew she had to leave and find her sister. She just didn't know how she was going to tell Keraun that.

"Yo, I fuckin' love you, baby girl." Keraun broke the silence.

Kim opened her eyes, but she didn't look at him.

"I always did. Now, tell me what's up. What really happened?" he followed up.

Kim shot up on the bed next to him. She started to tell him about the dudes in the hotel, the robbery, the car chase, but something told her not to. She shifted the conversation to the past. She had never really talked about how much she missed her parents. Kim finally opened up a little more and told Keraun that she always felt guilty about missing her parents, because she didn't want to make Aunt Lisa feel bad after she had sacrificed her young life to raise them. It was the first time Kim realized how angry she was that her parents were snatched away from her so young.

Keraun listened intently. He had fallen into his own form of deep thought.

"I just need to get to my sister so we can get out of this together," she said softly.

"I get it. Ain't no worries," Keraun assured. "I know she is all you got."

"Okay, but first promise me no matter what, you won't get in your feelings when I have to leave. I promise that as soon as this is all said and done, I will be back," Kim said.

Right away, Keraun started shaking his head.

Kim touched his face gently, and with love in her eyes, she said, "Donna is not the only person I have in the world. You are very important to me. I won't leave you for good. I just have to do this, and I'll be back. With your help, of course," she said with sincerity.

He seemed to contemplate what she was saying, then his tense facial expression softened. "A'ight. I'll help you in any way I can, but you need to keep your promise," Keraun told her. "I don't fall for chicks on the level I fell for you, baby girl."

"I will. I swear," Kim said, raising her right hand. She lay back down on his chest, relishing what could possibly be their last moments together.

Kim had tears in her eyes as she drove in the low-key, beat-up Honda Keraun gave her. The gun he gave her rested between her legs, and her mind couldn't get off of her last moments with him. She let out a long sigh and looked down at the dash to notice that she was practically out of gas. She finally pulled into a gas station right on the outskirts of Beaumont, Texas. She knew she still had hours before she reached New Orleans. Kim hadn't totally betrayed Donna. At least she was on her way to New Orleans like they'd planned, even if she was two days behind schedule.

Kim slowed the car down as she approached a light at the off ramp from the highway. She looked around, thinking, even in the country, there was no place like Texas in the world.

Across the street, she spotted a small, seedy motel that looked old as shit. She was so tired, she could barely keep her eyes open, so she decided she would check into the motel, no matter how terrible it was.

After she gassed up the Honda, she drove across the street and parked in the gravel parking area outside the motel. She grabbed the bag with the cash that Keraun had given her and headed inside the raggedy double doors that led to the lobby of the motel. It smelled like ass, old fried bologna, and strong-ass Pine-Sol cleaner. Kim's first instinct was to turn and get the fuck out of there, but her heavy eyelids and longing for some sleep propelled her forward to the front desk.

"Yeah?" a toothless front desk clerk grumbled.

What the fuck? Kim thought to herself. Every time the clerk spoke, a little bit of spit flew from his lips because he had no teeth. Kim moved side to side to make sure not one drop of his spit landed anywhere near her.

"A room. All cash," Kim mumbled, trying to keep her eye contact with the man to a minimum and trying to keep from getting rained on with his stale spit.

"Cash is fine," the man droned like he'd been saying the same thing all day. He reached behind him and took a key that was dangling on a scratched-up plastic keychain and handed it to Kim.

She looked at the key strangely and then back at the man. Now she was scared of what she would find inside the room at the old-ass, outdated motel.

"All set," the man said, licking his fingers as he peeled off the cash she had given him.

"Thanks," Kim grumbled. She was too tired at that point to protest or to drive any longer to find another spot.

Kim's room was on the first floor, which she didn't like. She was still paranoid about anyone busting in on her. She passed several addicts on her way to the room. There was some of everything going on at the motel. Clearly, it wasn't a place the police frequented, which worked for her. Kim noticed the barely dressed women milling about on the motel's outdoor tiers.

"Yuck," Kim mumbled to herself under her breath. Just the thought of those terrible-looking women selling sex made her stomach churn.

"Help!" A scream cut through the air as Kim made her way to her room.

Kim jumped and immediately went for her gun. She clutched tightly to her bag of cash.

"Help! He stole my shit!" The screams continued.

Kim whirled around on the balls of her feet, ready for whatever. Her eyes went round as she finally identified the source of the screams. She watched two fiends, a man and a woman, rolling around on the ground, fighting over a small bundle, which she assumed was crack or heroin.

Kim took a deep breath and shook her head as she finally made it to her room. This place was going to be worse than she thought, but there was no turning back now.

"I guess my ass won't be leaving the fucking room until I'm ready to bounce. A shower and some sleep is all I need; then I'm blowing this fucking joint," Kim told herself.

She entered the dark, dank room and shook her head in immediate disgust. She put on the weak little doorknob lock and the rusty chain to secure the door.

"I see my ass gonna need to keep my gun close. These locks ain't worth a shit," Kim said to herself. She threw bags down on the small, shabby little metal table inside the room and clicked on an old, lopsided lamp that sat next to the bed.

"What a dump," she said, looking around the room carefully. Everything inside looked like it was a throwback from the 1960s. The shag carpet was a horrible shade of orange. It looked like it hadn't been cleaned in centuries. The TV was one of those small, old-fashioned joints with the rabbit ear antennas, and it sat atop a cracked wood stand that seemed like one touch would cause it to collapse. The bed headboard was made of fabric bordered by dark wood, like something Kim had seen watching reruns of the old sitcoms with Donna and Aunt Lisa. The blanket on the bed looked like it had been there since before Kim was born. She snatched it off and threw it in the corner of the room, because no matter what, she wasn't sleeping on that shit.

Kim walked into the bathroom and noticed all the rust stains streaking the bottom of the tub. The shower curtain had mold stains streaking the bottom of it, and the toilet had rust stains in it as well.

"I need a shower, so this is just going to have to do," she told herself. Kim left her socks on, thinking she could ward off any fungus living in the bottom of the tub. She undressed, took a quick shower, and got in the bed. The sheets at least looked like they had been washed since the last person rented the room. She said a quick little prayer that she didn't get eaten alive by bedbugs and hoped for the best.

Kim turned on the TV, and of course, the news was on the one channel that worked. She turned up the volume when she noticed that the news crew was in front of Aunt Lisa's house. Kim squinted at the screen and couldn't stop watching what was playing.

"They really going off with this shit," Kim whispered. The reporters were talking to people that said they knew Donna, Kim, and Aunt Lisa. Kim laughed and shook her head in disgust at how easily people lied. Aunt Lisa had always warned Kim and Donna not to trust people. She used to say a so-called friend would turn on you faster than a stranger. Kim was seeing that shit firsthand. All those people that were down for them when they were riding high in designer threads and fast cars were the same people turning on them now. This was a prime example of everything Aunt Lisa had said. Kim always knew Aunt Lisa was wise beyond her years, and she couldn't help but feel guilty about the day she picked Keraun over her aunt and sister.

"It's crazy how you can't trust nobody these days. Even people you thought had your back were standing at your back with a knife," Kim spoke out loud in a disgusted tone as she watched person after person tell a different story about her and Donna. She didn't know that it was the least of what was in store for her.

Kim shut off the T.V. and counted out her money. She put a few dollars in her wallet and slid the bag containing the bulk of the money under the bed on the side where she planned to sleep. She thought about how she'd change up her look before she headed out, since now everybody wanted to be singing birds. After she prepared for the next day, it took no time for a heavy, deep sleep to overcome her.

Boom! The explosion of sound filled the room and violently ripped Kim out of a deep, deep sleep. She belched out a short-lived scream in response to the noise as her eyes popped open, sending a searing pain through her head. The motel room door crashing in almost gave her a heart attack. With her mind still fuzzy with sleep, Kim was on her feet within seconds. Instinctively, her hand went under the pillow and searched around. Kim's instincts were razor sharp. Even when she was resting, Kim was never really sleeping— another lesson from Aunt Lisa.

Donna had always thought of Kim as the weakest link. Kim knew this, and most of the time, being lazy, she played along. But she was just as sharp, or sharper, than her sister when it came to survival instincts. With the swiftness of a magician, Kim slid her hand under the pillow that next to the one she had been lying on. She locked her left hand around the weapon she'd gotten from Keraun and took a deep breath.

Kim could hear Donna's voice in her head: *Always be ready for anything.*

"Grab that bitch!" one of the goons growled as three men barged into Kim's room. The other two men lunged and came at Kim around the bed.

"She got a gun!" one of them screeched as the light was flicked on. The lead goon's eyes went wide, and his jaw dropped.

"I told you we needed to have our guns out! Shoot the bitch and let's go," one of the men complained.

"I thought they said she was a little girl. No need to attract attention to us with guns out coming up in here!" the lead goon gasped as he locked eyes with Kim. Fear flashed in his eyes, but fire flashed in hers.

Even with fear choking the shit out of her, Kim gritted. "Little girls kill too, bitch."

Boom! Without hesitation, one shot from Kim's gun dropped the leader of the goons.

"Who the fuck sent y'all?" Kim growled, leveling her gun at the other two cowering assholes as they tried to fumble for their guns. "Don't fucking make another move! Now, who the fuck sent y'all?" Kim said through her teeth.

Neither man said anything, but the one standing to the left threw up from the fear. When Kim saw that his fear had overcome him, she knew that he was the one she had to leave for last. Being a bitch who set niggas up for their ultimate downfall, Kim always knew how to exploit a dude's tiniest vulnerabilities. It was a skill she'd learned early on in life.

"I said, who the fuck sent y'all here? Who killed my fucking aunt and set us up?" Kim barked, trying her best to keep her galloping heart and the fire raging inside of her under control.

"Okay, you motherfuckers don't wanna say?" Kim said through clenched teeth. She stormed closer to the man on the right. "I guess y'all bitch-ass niggas don't wanna live, either."

"Stupid bit—" the man on the right started.

Boom! A direct shot to the temple sent the man's brain bursting out of the back of his skull. The vomit-faced coward that was on the left fell to his knees and began begging for his life.

"Please! Please don't kill me. I'll tell you who . . . who . . . sent us," he pleaded, tears falling from his eyes like a woman.

"Then talk, bitch nigga," Kim gritted, her gun dangling at her side. She smelled so much fear on the fake goon that she didn't even feel the need to keep her gun trained on him.

"It—it was . . ." the man stammered.

Kim squinted her eyes, waiting. "It was who? Talk, bitch!" All sorts of thoughts ran through Kim's mind as she waited.

"I'll tell you. Just put the gun away . . . please. Please, no one else needs to die."

"Who was it?" she barked at the terrified man.

"I can't tell you nothing when you holding that gun."

"You better start talking, or you gonna be laying right next to the lame asses on the floor. I ain't got time for this shit. Talk or you going to sleep!" Kim pointed the gun at him again. She wasn't about to let him think he was running the show.

"I—I'll nev—never tell," the man stammered.

Kim's mind was exploding with rage. "Well, then I guess you don't fucking want to live either," Kim said with finality. "Your loyalty got you killed. Remember that when you get to hell." One last shot, and she was done.

With her nerves on edge and the police surely on their way, Kim contemplated her next move. She gathered up the stuff she had on the table as fast as she could, but by mistake, in her haste, she left the cash she had stashed under the bed. It was the first in a series of mistakes that would come back to haunt her later.

Chapter 11

It had been a few days since Donna separated from Kim, and she was worried sick about her. She just had to hold out hope that her sister had taken the bus to New Orleans like she'd instructed. If she knew her sister like she thought she did, Kim had probably veered off the plan. Donna could only pray that wasn't true.

Donna was drifting in and out of sleep while she drove down the interstate. She kept shaking her head to stay awake. She couldn't afford to swerve or make a mistake and go over the speed limit and chance getting stopped by the cops. Moving in the thick of the night was her new thing.

Donna had never liked driving alone because once she got bored, she'd always start falling asleep. The news radio she was listening to wasn't helping either, but Donna had to stay tuned to the boring news station to listen for any new announcements about the manhunt for her and her sister. It felt like hours she'd been driving, but now she was only fifteen minutes from her destination.

She'd been a hypocrite for sure. She had preached hard and strong to Kim about not returning to Houston or anywhere near it, but Donna couldn't let this one go. She'd made it all the way past Beaumont, Texas, right before the Louisiana border, then turned around. Even with a manhunt and bounty out on her head, the itch of revenge was too strong not to scratch it. Her heart had been broken, and as risky as it was, Donna needed to right that wrong once and for all.

She looked down at the gas needle and sighed. It was that time. She needed gas, and she desperately had to piss. It was a risky undertaking, but it had to be done. Donna kept her eye out for a good place to stop. She wanted to pull over at a busy gas station instead of one that only had a few people in it. The fewer people, the more noticeable she would stand out. She figured the hat and glasses would help anyway.

Donna pulled into gas station right off of the highway. Before she got out, she checked herself out, making sure she could easily blend in. She looked like a nobody. She raced inside the gas station to use the bathroom, but before she could make it to the back where the restrooms were located, she noticed the television hanging up in the corner of the store. There they were, her and Kim, with their faces plastered on the damn news.

Donna looked around nervously. The store clerk was busy ringing up customers, and none of the other patrons had bothered to even look in Donna's direction as they went about picking up the items they intended to purchase.

Change of plans. Donna swiftly turned around and headed out the doors. She jumped back into the car and slowly drove out of the station.

"Close call, Donna. You've come too damn far to get caught up on some bullshit," she spoke to herself. It still blew her mind that the police were trying to say she and Kim had killed Aunt Lisa. If those asshole cops and the media only knew how much Kim and Donna both loved their aunt, there wouldn't even be a suspicion that they would harm one hair on Aunt Lisa's head. Donna got enraged just thinking about it.

She parked a few blocks up so she could program the GPS to take her to her next destination. She would have to find an alleyway to piss in and another gas station to get gas. Donna punched in the address she wanted.

"You don't know what you got coming," she whispered.

Something told her to let it go, but her heart and the thought of revenge kept her from being smart about it.

The further into Houston she drove, the more excited she got. It wasn't happy excitement; it was that deadly adrenaline-rush type of excitement. Donna couldn't wait to see the one person she just had to pay a visit to before she made her way to New Orleans. She hadn't even told Kim about her plan on this one, and she had no intentions of ever telling her sister about it.

Donna knew that Aunt Lisa would've warned her against going to deal with something like this alone, since she hadn't carefully prepared like she had been taught. Donna didn't care. She felt a gnawing urgency for revenge against this person, almost as much as she had felt for the bastards that ruined her family and took her parents away from her.

Donna couldn't focus on anything else until she paid a visit to Black, the man she once loved enough to betray her sister and Aunt Lisa for. She couldn't believe he had set her up like that. She had loved him and thought he would always love her. She had trusted him. It wasn't really her fault how shit had ended with them. Donna's nostrils flared just thinking about his betrayal. Her mind raced backward on her relationship with Black.

Summer 2014

"It's time for a new lick," Aunt Lisa announced.

Donna and Kim sat quietly, waiting for their instructions.

"I been hearing buck shit about a dude named Black s'posed to have the monopoly on the pills in the street.

Heard he's paid like a mu'fucka. I want y'all to get him.
Y'all know I hate a bragging mu'fucka too," Aunt Lisa
said. "Simple as that. We don't need a whole bunch of
discussion. Do what y'all were taught and get at him."

"Sounds like a plan to me," Kim said, already on her
feet and ready to make moves. She stretched her long,
lean frame and shimmied her slender hips.

"I'll leave this one to you. You're better at it than me
anyway," Donna said. She meant it. Kim was the prima
donna. She was better at using her assets than Donna
had ever been. Donna was fine giving the seducing part
over to Kim. She was way more interested in the setup
and takedown part of their licks anyway.

For a few days after they'd decided it was time for a
new move, Donna and Kim did their homework on this
Houston cat named Black, whose real name was Corey
Mills. Word on the streets was that Black had a lot of
the pill market in west Houston on lock. Rumor had it
he wasn't even from Houston but had trailed in from
Shreveport to set up shop.

"Outside niggas always coming to the H and trying to
exploit niggas. Acting like they ain't 'bout shit, but got
shit bubbling on the low. That's why I do what I do to
these niggas for real. They think they untouchable in
our fucking backyard. Fuck that!" Keraun had said to
Donna, Kim, and Aunt Lisa. They had all agreed with that
assessment. Long before Donna laid actual eyes on Black,
she hated him.

But the day Donna actually laid eyes on the man she
learned was the infamous Black, she had to do a double
take. The nigga was fine as hell! Donna had never in her
life seen a man so fine with absolutely no flaws at all. A
lot of the dudes she cased were usually ugly but dressed
nice, or if they were fine, they usually wore corny-ass
clothes. Donna had never seen the best of both—Black

was fine, and his clothes were so well put together and hitting that she was stunned.

With her jaw almost on the floor, Donna stared at Black, drinking in all of his features, and she immediately started fantasizing about him. Donna let all sorts of thoughts race through her mind as her pussy thumped a little bit. Shit, she was feeling things down low that she hadn't ever felt by just looking at a dude.

Black stood six feet two inches tall; had broad, basketball-player shoulders; the smoothest dark skin Donna had ever seen; and slick, jet black, soft curls of hair that hugged his head like an Indian straight from India. Donna watched him, and when he smiled, flashing his perfect white teeth, Donna felt her pulse quicken, even from a distance. Donna had never really found herself physically attracted to anyone like that before. She didn't think anyone could tell, but the person who knew her best was watching her while she watched Black.

"I thought you was leaving this one up to me. Your ass 'bout to fall over staring and drooling. Don't be falling in love. That nigga is our next hit, so don't be looking at him like you wanna eat him whole," Kim joked the night she and Donna first saw Black.

"Aunt Lisa will be pissed if we mess this up. This nigga look like he got long paper," Kim said.

"Shut up, Kim. You don't know me like you think you do. I don't even like him," Donna snapped defensively. She silently scolded herself and made it up in her mind that Black was just their next lick, not a nigga she liked. Period. It was mind over matter, or so she thought.

For some reason, Kim gave it up. She told Donna the setup was on her, and Aunt Lisa agreed. Donna was a little pissed with Kim, but secretly she was glad. There was just something about that damn Black that she liked to watch. Donna volunteered to set up the lick on Black, partly because she wanted to see him again without the scrutiny of Kim, but also because Donna figured if Kim went with her, there would be too much for Black to choose from and shit might go awry with the lick. Donna wasn't going to act like she didn't know Kim was gorgeous, a fact that no one around them ever tried to deny. Donna knew that Kim had a way of capturing dudes as soon as they laid eyes on her. This was going to be Donna's opportunity to show that she could pull a fine dude too.

Aunt Lisa, Kim, and even Keraun had given Donna so many instructions that Donna wanted to run away. In the end, Donna understood that her job was to find out everything about Black—where he lived, where he hung out, who his right-hand man was, who his enemies were, his full government name, his relationship status, where his family was from, where they laid their heads, how he did business, and most importantly, what he was holding and where he kept most of his stash. Aunt Lisa and Keraun considered themselves experts at this shit; therefore, they never carried out a lick without first conducting extensive research on all their victims. But this would be Donna's first time going it alone. She had to make sure she did it well, or else she'd be embarrassed and upstaged by her sister, who was already known to be able to snag any lick.

After driving to the other side of town, Donna pulled her rental car into the Courtyard Marriot. She wanted to be as close as possible to where Black allegedly ran his business. She checked into her room under the alias Deja Veux. Aunt Lisa always had them use fake names when they were researching a lick. They hardly used their real names for much of anything.

As soon as Donna kicked off her heels, she called Kim to let her and Aunt Lisa know she was in.

"Keep that fucking phone close when you go out there," Aunt Lisa demanded through the phone. "We need to know your moves. No bullshit. We want to be updated and keep tabs on your well-being at all times. I am not playing with you, girl," Aunt Lisa said with feeling.

Donna rolled her eyes, thinking Aunt Lisa was always over the top with her protectiveness. It got on Donna's nerves to no end.

After she spoke to Aunt Lisa, Kim, and Keraun and went over the plan for what seemed like the hundredth time, Donna took a long, hot shower, relaxed in her hotel room, and got her mind right for the mission at hand. She laid out a royal blue, close-fitting Donna Karan pantsuit, a pair of silver Saint Laurent heels, and a white-and-silver YSL clutch. Every single thread had come from Kim. Donna was more of a sneaker head, but her usual style would've never worked for the mission at hand. It was well known that hustling dudes wanted trophies on their arms. Donna had to be a trophy. In her assessment, the high-end designer threads were probably overkill for anywhere she would be hanging out in the hood, but according to her lesson from Kim, that was the look Donna was going for—definite overkill. She had watched Black long enough to figure he would probably only be seen with chicks that had their shit all the way together in the clothes, hair, and body departments. Every time she had laid eyes on him, he had been in nothing less than the best threads.

Donna had no worries about herself when it came to the designer clothes, beauty, hair, and body departments. She may not have considered herself as beautiful as Kim, but Donna knew she was a beauty too. Where she was from, just like her sister, all the dope boys wanted her, and all the hood chicks hated her.

That first night, Donna knew exactly what spot she'd be hitting up first. Thanks to good research, Donna pulled up to club Venue on Main Street and let the valet park her car. Judging by the crowd outside, Venue seemed to be the place to be that night, just like she had heard. Donna had already gotten the scoop from a kid named Buggs that worked for Keraun that Black might've been a partial owner of Venue.

The outside of the club was nothing to look at. It was a nondescript brick building that looked more like a warehouse from the front than a club. Once Donna saw how long the line was outside the club, she knew standing on it wasn't her damn style. In all their days of casing licks, Donna and Kim didn't wait on lines, and certainly not when they were as dressed up in the best shit like Donna was that night. She decided that she was too spoiled, too beautiful, and too smart to be looking hungry and thirsty on some club line.

Donna made the decision that it was time for her to get her game face on and use the gaming skills she had acquired over the years to get herself inside. Shit, if she could game niggas right out of their stacks, getting in the club shouldn't be problem at all, she told herself.

Donna smoothed her dress down over her round backside and took a deep breath before she sauntered toward the club's doors. Her heels clicked against the pavement with a nice smooth cadence. She had learned how to walk in heels from Aunt Lisa. That was a fact that still made Donna kind of sad. These were all things that she should've learned from her mother.

Donna approached the door, focused on her mission. Surprisingly, there was only one lame, overweight, trying-to-look-hard weakling bouncer at the front door.

Oh, this shit gonna be easier than I thought. This lame don't stand a chance against me, she said to herself, building up her own confidence. Donna had already caught the portly wannabe-tough bouncer looking at her like she was a pulled pork sandwich, so she knew if she played her cards right, she would have this one in the bag.

"Hey, you," Donna sang, smiling sweetly. "You look like you could use some company out here. Listen, I forgot my pass, but Black is expecting me, so I trust that you're going to move aside and let me right up in here." Donna licked her shiny lips and smiled brightly, flashing all of her perfectly straight teeth.

"Black ain't tell me nothing about expecting you, though," the bouncer wheezed, sweat beads sliding down his face and making a pool near his neckline. He couldn't even hold eye contact with Donna—a good sign for her.

She looked him up and down. She was disgusted, but she smiled anyway. She was praying she wouldn't have to touch him to make it better.

"Well, I'm telling you Black is expecting me, hun. I'm sorry you're not having a great night. I'm not either. I was rushing out after getting all dressed up and forgot the pass, Tuh, my fault for trying to be so sexy tonight," Donna said, sliding her hand down over her ample ass to entice the portly bouncer.

"You see what I see?" Donna said seductively. Then she winked at the bouncer. "I may not have the pass Black gave me, but I know the password," Donna said sexily, licking her lips for emphasis.

"Pleeease," Donna said in a sexy moan that could've easily been in a soundtrack to a porn movie. "I know you like to see a beautiful woman dressed to the nines with this sexy body get in, and all because of you. I know you wanna see me inside and maybe grab these digits later. And get some kudos from Black at the same time, once I tell him you looked out," she breathed, speaking like she was having phone sex. With that, she moved so close to the fat man that he could smell the mint IceBreakers on her breath and the enticing scent of her Gucci Envy perfume. This was definitely not her personality style, but she'd watched Kim use this method so many times it was as if she had already done it herself.

"*Please* is the password, and this is the key." She breathed like she was on the verge of orgasm, then she reached down and grabbed a handful of the bouncer's musty crotch. Although his dick must've been tiny because she still couldn't feel it, he got the message she was sending.

Donna was so disgusted by the damp spot on his pants, but she couldn't quit now. She was all the way in now. She kept asking herself, *what would Kim do? What would Kim do?* And she knew the answer. Kim would make that fat-ass bouncer feel like he was the man to get whatever she wanted. Donna kept at it, even though her stomach was turning with disgust.

"Oh, shit," the bouncer panted, clearly beside himself. It was as if he had run a million blocks. He didn't even care that the desperate clubgoers on the line were yelling at him and cussing Donna out for skipping the line.

Donna figured his fat ass probably hadn't been touched down there by a woman in years, so she stroked what little she could feel. "Oh, is that a banana in your pants or you just happy to see me? Now, you don't want Black to find out how you sexually harassed me out here in public, do you?" Donna whispered. "How you made me rub your dick to get inside, knowing that I am his special friend. I don't think you want me to tell your boss all about how this went down," Donna said in a baby voice.

"Okay, okay," the man said, finally relenting. As he stepped aside, his entire body was trembling from sexual excitement. He could not take her another minute. He looked like wanted to throw her down and fuck her right there."I–I'ma let you inside, bu–but you will need this to show the other security inside," the bouncer said, handing Donna a real VIP pass.

Damn, I'm good! Aunt Lisa definitely ain't raise no slouches! she thought. She had made up the story about leaving the pass at home, not even knowing that the club really used passes.

Donna took her lucky entry into the club as a sign from God that she was meant to be there that night, casing the joint and Black for their next lick.

Once inside, Donna took in an eyeful of the club. It was decked out with beautiful black tiled floors, a lot of glass walls and tables, beautiful faux crystal chairs, and silver benches that could double for glass if you didn't know any better. The dim lighting around the ceiling and floor of the club cast a sexy glow across the entire dance floor. The interior made Donna think of something her parents would've liked. They had always had a penchant for extravagance.

She could tell it was still early. Some people were sitting on the benches, all sophisticated-like, with expensive cocktails in their hands and expensive bottle service bottles on ice in front of them. Some were moving their bodies on the dance floor, and others were posted up around the walls, people watching.

Donna slid onto one of the barstools and ordered a Henny and coke. She ended up sitting at the bar inside the club for two hours before Black finally arrived. When he came in, Donna noticed how the floor opened up to allow him to walk through. It was what she imagined the parting of the Red Sea looked like.

Black wasn't hard to notice, and just like she remembered, he was still fine as hell. Even in the darkened club, Donna could still see those perfect white teeth shining and that gleaming skin. That night, Black rocked a simple pair of dark jeans, a white Louis Vuitton V-neck, and a pair of black alligator skin Buscemi high-top sneakers. Donna was wooed all over again. Seeing Black made any doubts she'd had fade right away.

Donna also immediately noticed all the chicks swooning over Black. They were all set and ready to pounce. Donna decided to do it differently. She had a lot of competition, and there was one thing Aunt Lisa always preached: never jockey with another bitch for a lick's attention. If he ain't interested, move on.

Donna played it cool and acted like Black's presence didn't mean shit to her. She was watching, though. Donna knew that niggas like Black always watched for the chicks that weren't interested. They always wanted the one they felt would be a challenge. That plan could either work or backfire. Either way, that night, Donna was taking a chance.

After almost three hours in the club and about four snifters of Hennessy and Coke, Donna was tipsy, frustrated, feeling useless, and ready to call it a night. She was beating herself up, saying she should've let her sister take this one. Donna felt like she wasn't attractive enough to snag Black. Her buzz had begun to wear off, and so had her self-esteem. She was all dressed up like she was about to hit the red carpet, and Black hadn't even glanced at her from what she could tell.

Donna had watched him long enough to assess that his aura and demeanor were different than any other dudes she had come across, especially the ones she and Kim had cased for a lick over the years. All the hustlers she and Kim had made their victims were usually flashy, loud, careless, and downright stupid. They were so interested in showing and telling people what they had and living that social media life that most of them never thought far ahead about the predators that might be after their shit. Black had proven himself to be different. He was laid back, not flashy at all. Donna watched all of Black's crew being loud and boisterous, but not him. He was cool, calm, and collected the entire time. He was seemingly uninterested in anyone around him.

Donna's mind raced with all sorts of thoughts, but she wasn't ready to give up just yet. She was determined to make him notice her. Even if he didn't bite as a lick, she just needed to know that she could snag a nigga like Black. She was worried that Kim would always get all the good men, and she would be left with the shit.

After another hour, nothing. Donna was just about to leave the club, feeling dejected, when she noticed one of Black's crew walking toward her. He was the dude she'd seen whispering to Black that night. He was also the dude that kept coming to the bar and kind of watching her. At first, Donna just knew he was going to try to push up and fuck up her whole plan, but he never did.

As the dude got closer to her, Donna's body tensed up. She set down her drink and waited. Sure enough, just like she suspected, Black's dude approached her.

"You good?" the dude asked.

She nodded, but not enough for him to say she had answered his question.

"Never seen you here before," the dude said, his Rolex diamond bezel threatening to blind her.

"First time," Donna said.

"You good, though? You acting like me talking to you is a problem," the dude said. "My name is Quay. I'm trying to get to know you," he said.

Donna's entire body got hot. She had been hoping he'd say something like "My boss wanted me to ask you over" or "My boss is interested," not for him to ask her out.

"I don't want to be known," Donna said almost through her teeth. But then, just like a bolt of lightning, something hit her. Whatever she had to do to get close to Black might work, even talking to this dude.

Quay laughed. "You a mean one," he said. "You can't even give a nigga a chance?"

She didn't care what he was talking about. She was still trying to figure how she'd use him to hatch a plan against Black.

"How about I meet up with you sometime this week? Take my number. Let me know where you and your friends hang out, and I'll catch up to you," Donna said slyly. She was going to have to play this whole thing just right. So far, everything had been going wrong.

"Shit. I'm there!" Quay said, smiling like a big kid.

Donna smirked and rolled her eyes as he rushed away. "Yeah, right, nigga. I wouldn't give you the time of day," Donna mumbled as she hopped down from the barstool and stomped toward the exit. The night definitely hadn't gone as she expected. This was going to be a lot more work than she'd anticipated.

For the next week, Donna used Quay to her advantage. Like a gossiping-ass female, Quay told Donna everywhere that Black and his people were hanging out each night. If she hadn't been so enamored with him, Donna could've called Keraun and Aunt Lisa and the crew and got Black good a few times because of his boy's blabbing.

Thanks to Quay, Donna had been to clubs, bars, and even bowling alleys dressed in the hottest high-end labels, with perfect makeup and hair, trying to get Black's attention. Still, no matter how hot Donna looked and how many other dudes swooned over her, Black seemed to pay her no mind. Donna was growing frustrated, but at the same time, slowly more and more attracted to Black. It was his smooth-ass vibe and perfect demeanor that had Donna open. Something about Black had her intrigued like never before. He kind of reminded her of her father—so smooth a person never knew what he was thinking or what his next move might be, like a master chess player.

The thing that baffled Donna the most, though, was how skillfully Black ignored her. She couldn't understand why he didn't even blink in her direction. It was like every hustler in Texas had come after her since she'd arrived on the scene, but the one person she wanted to chase her still hadn't said as much as hello to her.

"What's up, sis?" Kim answered her phone on the first ring.

Donna had her lips poked out and her foot tapped against the floor. "Something is up. I can't get next to this nigga Black for shit," Donna complained, biting down on her lip hard.

"What's going on? He hasn't pushed up?" Kim asked incredulously.

"No! He hasn't even tried to look my way. I see mad bitches swirling, but it's like he ain't interested in none of them either. I say the nigga married and faithful or gay as fuck," Donna replied, clearly upset.

"You know this is game, right? Give it one more day. I'm telling you, he's pressed, but he trying to see what you gonna do. He notices your frustration. Stay off the scene for a few days," Kim said, speaking from experience.

"You know how those big timers do. They act like they ain't interested, but that's just to see how frustrated you get. I hope you playing it cool like Aunt Lisa taught us, because that nigga probably watching your every move and you just don't know it. Be careful that he don't figure you out, too. Keep playing that innocent role and see what happens," Kim continued.

Donna cringed. She hated being lectured by her little sister.

"I know better. I'm not going to be like these bitches throwing themselves at him, but for real, a nigga starting to fuck with my self-esteem," Donna continued complaining. "I mean, if this is a game, that nigga got game for days, because he all up in my head space."

"You better stop talking crazy. You're fucking gorgeous. Mommy and Daddy ain't make no ugly kids. You don't need a nigga to chase you to prove it, so stop it. He playing games. One more day and see what's up. I won't even tell Aunt Lisa and Keraun we had this conversation. You know what to do. This ain't your first time at the rodeo, Donna." With that, Kim hung up.

Donna flopped back on her hotel room bed, frustrated. She was feeling Black a lot, and the fact that every time he even glanced her way it was like she was invisible to him was really sending her crazy.

The next morning, Donna decided that she needed to change shit up. She thought a few new items of clothing would make her at least feel better about herself since Black's blatant disregard had started taking a little toll on her self-esteem. Donna headed out for some much-needed pampering.

A couple hours later, dressed in a close-fitting Victoria's Secret Pink sweatsuit, with no makeup on and her hair thrown up in a high, messy bun, Donna examined her newly manicured nails. It wasn't the quality of work she was used to from their private nail technician, but it would do until she could get back home.

After paying the manicurist, Donna carefully threaded her wrists through the handles of all the shopping bags she had acquired from her trip to the mall and headed out of the nail salon. As she made her way to her car, she noticed a black G-Wagen moving slowly through the parking lot in her direction. Her guard immediately went up as the Benz truck continued to creep up on her. Turning to face off with the driver, Donna stopped at her car, let the bags on her wrists fall to the ground, and grabbed her purse where her gun was inside. If a nigga was going to run up on her, he was certainly going to get more than he bargained for. With her head tilted to the side as if to say "bring it, nigga," Donna waited, eyes squinted and her hand on her pistol.

The G-Wagen slowed to a halt right in front of her, and the dark-tinted passenger-side window slowly went down. Donna was already mean-mugging and waiting.

"Somebody said you been following me. Is that true?" Black said smoothly from the driver's seat.

Donna's heart almost leapt up out of her chest as soon as she laid eyes on Black's gorgeous, smiling face. She moved her hand from her purse, and she could feel the tension easing out of her face. She squinted against the sun and looked into his vehicle. Black was alone, which was a first in the time Donna had been watching him.

"Why would I be following you? Are you important or something?" Donna retorted, playing it off. Meanwhile, her insides were jumping for joy.

Black laughed.

"It ain't funny." She smiled, unable to keep a serious face while looking at his.

"You're the new girl on the scene everybody talking about, huh? I been seeing you around, but you always look so serious, like you ain't tryna give a nigga no play," Black said lightheartedly, with a smooth baritone that sounded like music to Donna's ears.

"I wouldn't say I'm new, just different," she came back sassily. Then she winked to let him know she was playing.

"Nah, you new. I'm the king of this side of town. I know who's new and who's old," he replied, rubbing his neatly lined goatee.

Donna felt like she could just faint. If love at first sight was a thing, this was it.

"King?" Donna laughed.

Black laughed too. "King. So, where you headed? I might be looking for a date," he said, flashing that panty-dropper smile.

Donna was beside herself. Her stomach was doing flips, her toes were balled up in her Gucci sneakers, and she was clenching her ass cheeks together so hard they were trembling a little bit. Black couldn't tell, though, because Donna was a master a keeping a poker face and appearing to keep her cool. It was another skill she'd learned from Aunt Lisa.

"It's a good thing I'm hungry," she answered.

Black got out of his truck, walked over, picked up Donna's bags, threw them in his back seat, and opened his passenger-side door for her. That just made her even more hooked.

"First, I need to go change. I'm not dressed to go out," Donna said, touching her messy hair.

"Psh. No need to change for me. I already know how good you look all dressed up. Like I said, I've seen you for a few days now. I did notice you. I think you're more beautiful without all of the makeup and fancy shit," Black told her.

Donna inadvertently let a smile slip across her lips, all the while her heart was beating wildly in her chest. She had never really dated anyone. The few times she'd snuck around with dudes, Aunt Lisa always found a way to dead it before it could really blossom into anything serious.

"So, your mother named you Black?" Donna said sarcastically as they drove away.

He started laughing. "Nah, my name is Brice, but only my special friends and family call me by my government."

"Good . . . Brice, I'm Donna. It's nice to meet you," she said boldly. Just like that, things changed for Donna.

For the next five days, Black showed Donna a good time. They went to high-priced dinners, he showed her all the spots he owned, including two strip clubs, he sent flowers to her hotel, and he even took her apartment hunting after she lied and told him she was looking to move. Their time together was light and devoid of tension. It was really like nothing Donna had ever experienced; especially because most of her dates were based on setting dudes up and being fake.

It was so easy to be around Black that Donna almost forgot he was supposed to be her next victim. She felt totally different around him. Her palms would sweat, her heart raced, her brain was stimulated like never before, and something was definitely going on between her legs. Donna had asked herself a few times if this was what love felt like.

Donna was falling for Black, and the more she did, the less she wanted to go through with setting him up. Nothing convinced her more than one night when she accidentally fell asleep at Black's condo without a care in the world. She awoke, and as soon as her eyes cracked open to her surroundings, panic immediately hit her like a ton of bricks falling from the sky. She popped up in Black's bed and looked around wildly. A cold sweat had broken out all over her body, and she instinctively reached around for her purse where her gun was kept. Donna cursed under her breath when she realized it was the next morning and she was still at Black's house and in his bed.

"How could you be so stupid?" she scolded herself.

Donna looked around but didn't see Black. His Cartier watch, iPhone, and wallet were all on the nightstand on the opposite side of the bed. That told her that he probably hadn't left the condo, but where was he, she wondered.

"Aunt Lisa would fucking kill you if she knew you let your guard all the way down like this," Donna grumbled to herself as she gathered her clothes. If she was going to stay the night, that would've required notification to Kim, Aunt Lisa, and Keraun for her safety. Donna felt stupid.

The night before, when Black had invited Donna to his condo, they had a few drinks, but she had not allowed herself to get drunk—or so she thought. She remembered laying on Black's chest and talking to him into the wee hours of the morning, but what stuck out to her most was that he hadn't even tried to have *sex* with her. Black had been a perfect gentleman that night. In fact, in Donna's eyes, he was a perfect man for her, not to mention fine and paid. He had shared with her that he owned just as many legitimate businesses as he did illegal ones. He had no kids. But, whenever he had them, he wanted a big family. That had endeared Donna to Black even more. She wanted a big family too. When they talked about their childhoods, Black shared that his parents had been hustlers just like him, but they had both died when he was younger.

Things had gotten deep between Black and Donna, but not so deep that she shared that much about herself with him at that time. She did, however, tell him that her parents had just disappeared when she and Kim were younger, and that Aunt Lisa was their rock.

Donna had decided at that moment that she wanted to know Black on a different level, so she had taken him off her list of victims to rob. Now she would have to convince Kim and Aunt Lisa that Black wasn't a good target. That was going to be the hard part.

"Good morning," Black said cheerfully as he walked into the bedroom with a tray of food. "I cooked you some breakfast," he said, flashing his winning, heart-melting smile.

Donna quickly forgot her dilemma and was back to feeling loved. "You cooked it?" she laughed, twisting her lips. Suddenly, she wasn't in a rush to leave anymore, and she instantly forgot about Kim and Aunt Lisa and their impending lecture.

"Busted! My chef cooked it, but I told her exactly what to cook," Black relented. "See, all for you, picked out by me."

He and Donna both busted out laughing. She was having the time of her life. There was not one thought of why she had really been there.

That morning, Donna and Black shared breakfast on the terrace outside of his bedroom like they were a married couple. It was like a scene from a romance movie. Donna was caught up. She realized she had never felt love prior to meeting Black. He was a real man, and she was falling in real love with him.

While they shared breakfast, Black and Donna engaged in more deep conversation. This time Black told her he was looking for a good girl to settle down with. He spoke about all the trouble he had been going through finding a woman that wasn't either scheming on him for money or setting him up for the downfall. Donna was immediately plagued by guilt. She had definitely been setting him up for the downfall.

"I gotta take a trip for a few days, Black," Donna announced in a disappointed tone. As badly as she wanted to stay, she knew she had to break up their little thing, or else she might never go back. Any man that had Donna contemplating betraying Kim and Aunt Lisa had definitely taken hold of her heart, and she knew it. It was a dangerous emotion that she hadn't experienced before.

"Damn, I thought you was mine for good," Black replied, disappointed.

"I'll be back. I promise you that. It's just I found out there was some old business I need to handle," Donna lied. For the first time in her life, she felt bad for lying.

"Let me take you and bring you back then," Black told her with apprehension in his voice. He looked so sad and dejected that she was leaving. Donna could tell he didn't believe she would be back. She could also tell Black was feeling her just as much as she was feeling him.

"I would let you take me, but I definitely have to handle this on my own. I promise I'll be back," Donna said with feeling. She meant every word she said, too. Black was the one for her. Donna was definitely in love.

Donna returned home with a ready story in her head for Aunt Lisa and Kim. Her mind was consumed with Black. She took several deep breaths before she walked into her house.

"Well, if it isn't Miss Set-his-ass-up herself," Aunt Lisa joked as soon as she laid eyes on Donna.

"Hey, Auntie." Donna flashed a fake smile, but her stomach was in knots. It seemed like Aunt Lisa and Kim had been expecting her. Donna was wracked with guilt, fearing she would disappoint them. Anticipation was written all over their faces. In their minds, money talked and bullshit walked.

"What info you got? Shit, I need some paper," Kim said without even really properly greeting Donna.

"Wow. No greeting, nothing. I'm happy to see you too, Kim," Donna retorted.

"Stop whining, crazy. I am happy to see your ass. We just been waiting to know what's up with this next lick. You act like you don't want money just as bad as we do," Kim said, defending herself.

Donna knew Kim was right. She clenched her toes tight in her kicks and prepared herself to tell the biggest lie of her life. "Well, ain't nothing up with it. It's a dead issue. That dude ain't about it like that," Donna lied with a straight face. Her heart was running a race inside her chest.

"What?" Aunt Lisa asked, shooting Donna a death stare.

"Yeah. I was fucked up when I found out, too. That nigga Black ain't got no business like that. Our intel was wrong. He ain't worth our time," Donna lied some more.

It was like she had just told them she was dying or something. Aunt Lisa lit a cigarette. She only smoked when she was stressed out. Donna knew that meant the information had to be believable.

"We were wrong about him. I was there. I hung out and got close to him. He's definitely not what we thought. He ain't worth our time." The more she lied, the easier it became to believe what she was saying. She had never pegged herself as a chick that would lie to her family over no dude, but there she was, lying like shit.

"Nah. You're wrong. I heard he real big time," Kim interjected suspiciously.

Donna rolled her eyes at Kim. She wanted so badly to tell her sister to shut up before Aunt Lisa really started pressing her.

"I know what you think from the one or two times you seen him, but like I said, I saw it with my own eyes. He ain't about shit. In fact, it looked to me like he was a flunky. It would be more trouble than it's worth. I didn't even see who he works for, but he definitely don't work for himself," Donna said, trying like hell to sell her story.

"So, you trying to say Keraun's peoples were lying about this nigga?" Aunt Lisa pressed.

"Basically," Donna mumbled.

Kim sucked her teeth. "I knew I should've taken this one. This was way too important, and she ain't used to moving in on real niggas," Kim blurted.

"Shut the hell up!" Donna boomed. "Don't try to play me. I did what I needed to do, and I said the nigga ain't about shit."

"Hmph. Yeah, okay. The real story gonna come out one day," Kim grumbled.

"Fuck you, Kim!"

"Hey! None of that bullshit!" Aunt Lisa interjected. "Since when we fight over a simple-ass lick? Naw, we move the fuck on. If the nigga ain't about shit, it's time to move on to the next plan," Aunt Lisa said, blowing out her smoke. Donna's tensed muscles eased with relief as soon as Aunt Lisa agreed to move to another potential victim. Donna could see that Kim was still suspicious, but Kim alone didn't run the show.

After that worked out, Donna had to figure out a way to keep seeing Black on the low. She knew she would have to be careful, or her lie would be revealed, and Aunt Lisa would lose her shit. Donna was determined, because for the first time in her life, she was in love.

Donna swiped roughly at the tears that were falling from her eyes like an open faucet as she remembered those days. She had bitten the inside of her cheek until she drew blood, just thinking about how she'd met and fell in love with Black; how she'd lied to her family for him. It wasn't her fault he'd gotten locked up and lost everything. What had he expected her to do? She couldn't visit and make their relationship public back then. She'd kept his commissary books stacked and inched in a visit every now and again, but not enough to raise any eyebrows. They'd drifted apart as a couple, but damn, she thought they'd always have love for each other. Black had become one of her best friends even after prison had faded their love story. Donna had never expected his betrayal, and he had to pay.

She could still remember the feeling of hurt when she figured out it was Black that had made it possible for those dudes to bust up in the hotel and assault and rob her and Kim. After that day, she prayed daily that she would have the opportunity to find out where he was laying low, so that she could see him one last time.

Donna had been overjoyed when one of her boys got the intel for her. It had been risky reaching out to anyone in the streets, but Donna was that determined. She had cried when she thought about it all, and how she was going to handle it. Where she came from, she had no choice. Finding Black had given Donna a second wind and a new will to get back to her sister. The revenge was pushing her, motivating her.

Now, she stood in front of the address, feeling a stomach-sickening mix of emotions. Donna knew Black had always liked luxury. She also knew that, as cool as he had tried to play it in the past, Black never liked to be without a woman to call his own. She ran her fingers across the gun she had in the pocket of the oversized jacket she'd stolen as she thought about how she would do this. All she needed to do was be smart, fast, and careful. Keeping the emotions out of it was going to be the challenge. Donna was well aware that love didn't just dissipate with time. She still loved him.

Donna crept to the back of the small house. The block was quiet. She hadn't seen many people out all morning. She said a silent prayer, keeping her head down and her face covered, just in case any nosey neighbors ventured out into their back yards.

He said the big blue pot had the key, Donna recited to herself, remembering the information her boy had given her.

"Perfect," Donna huffed as she retrieved the key. At the back door, she stopped for a few seconds and took three deep, mind-clearing breaths. She sucked in a deep one at the end and felt like she had the courage of a superhero.

"You can do this. You have to do this," she whispered, her words coming out jagged due to her nerves.

Donna slipped the key into the door and carefully turned it until she heard a tiny click. She felt sweat running a race down the sides of her face. As she stepped into the quiet house, her nerves were on edge. Her legs felt like they'd buckle under her at any minute.

She stopped moving and tried to still her breathing. She listened for any sounds and could finally hear the faint drone of a television coming from upstairs. The hairs on her neck and arms stood up.

Motherfucker! Donna swallowed hard and silently rattled off in her head what she had come to do.

Then she thought, *It's not like Black not to have security cameras.*

Finally, she heard movement above her. A door slammed, and Donna almost fainted from nerves. She moved to a side wall and hid.

"Petey?" Black called out from the top of the stairs. "Yo, nigga, that you?"

Donna's heart felt like it would bust through her chest as she heard Black's footsteps getting closer. She could do one of two things—come out shooting, or wait, play it off, and confront him first. She decided to handle it the way her heart told her to handle it.

"Hey, Black," Donna cooed, stepping from the wall and into his eyesight. His eyes went wide. "Yo, what the—how you . . . what are you doing here?" Black stammered, shock filtering across his face and the edginess of nerves creaking into his voice.

Donna blinked for a few seconds before her brain sent the right message to her tongue. "Why you so surprised to see me?" she asked, smiling wickedly. She had him. There he stood, in his boxers and a wife beater, no gun and nowhere to run.

"I . . . I'm just wondering how you got in here," Black said, trying to play it cool. He knew if he retreated up the steps, he'd look weak; but he also knew he couldn't trust the situation, since Donna had seemingly broken into his spot.

"I have my ways," she said, followed by a sinister laugh. This persona was more Kim than Donna, but Donna had learned the tricks.

"So, what's up? You came here just for a social call?" Black asked, tilting his head to the side and rubbing his chin like he always did when he was calculating his next move. In the past, Donna had loved that about him—his calculating mind.

"I came to find you, so we can clear the air. You know I always had mad love for you, but you wanted to believe something different, so you let feelings get in the way of your good judgment," Donna said, her voice cracking with fake despair. She had made sure to get rid of her emotions before coming face to face with Black. This was all an act.

Donna could see in Black's eyes that he knew exactly what she was referring to.

"I don't know what you're talkin' about," Black lied.

Donna let out a long breath. Now he was insulting her intelligence. Her first thought was to just shoot him dead, right there, but she had come there for revenge, and revenge required a little more suffering.

"C'mon. We both know that ain't true, Black. You had a point to prove when I reached out to you for help, and you came back to prove it," she said. "I'm not mad. I just had to see you, though. The love . . . it's not gone. No matter what happened, how many hurts, I still love you."

Black lowered his gaze and sat back on the step. "Yo, I ain't never love no chick like I love you. That's on my life. You was really the love of my life. That shit devastated me when I came home and couldn't be with you."

A mixture of hurt and excitement flitted through Donna's stomach, causing her to feel lightheaded. She knew he loved her. That's why she still couldn't understand what he'd done.

"Well, I'm headed out of Texas for good, and I needed to see you one last time," Donna said.

Black looked at her suspiciously. "I thought you'd be gone by now. Word on the streets is you're wanted for your aunt's murder, and some real important people are after you."

Donna nodded her head. "So I heard. What about you? You think I would do something like that?" Donna asked, moving closer to Black in a lustful way. She could hear his breathing getting deeper.

"Well, you changed. I don't know what to say you would do," he said in a low, lust-filled baritone.

"You know damn well I wouldn't hurt my aunt," Donna gritted. She was trying to hold on to her composure again.

Black put his hands up and got up from the step. "It's all love. I ain't the cops. You know I got love for you, D." He eyed her up and down and licked his lips. "Why don't we go upstairs? I'm home alone. This is your going away—our final closure. Ain't like we didn't have good times in the past. I still think about back then," he said, moving close to her. He figured she was there for revenge, but he wasn't going to let her get the jump on him. He was going to be smarter than her.

Donna could smell him. It was the familiar scent that had sealed the deal on her feelings for him back in the day. She felt her heart trying to take over her head. She felt her body wanting to betray her. It was like torture.

"I always had love for you," Black said, the warmth of his breath next to her ear.

Donna felt her nervousness and fear fading into a fiery nugget of lust, but she had to stay focused on the plan. She stepped backward a few steps.

"You know I always wanted to say that it wasn't my fault the way shit played out with us. I just had to do what I had to do. I didn't know what your circumstances were going to be when you touched back down, or *if* you ever would. You should've talked to me, and I would've explained it," Donna said, her voice catching in her throat a few times. "You were the only man I've ever loved." Donna bit her lip to keep herself from screaming out. She really had to fight back the feelings threatening to make her abort her plan and run for the door. It was too late now. She was caught up.

"For real? Me? Nah. You liked the idea of me, but I don't know if that was love," Black said, now his voice was gruff with feeling.

Donna shook her head. She shouldn't have gone there. This was too much. She didn't even know what it was inside of her that was keeping her from just pulling her gun at that moment and blowing Black's head off.

"You know it was love. You know you broke my—" Donna huffed but never got to finish.

Black moved in on her and covered her mouth with his. She tried to protest, but she was no match for his size. They tussled for a few seconds, and she finally got too tired to fight.

Donna melted against him. He hoisted her onto him and carried her upstairs. She wasn't even thinking about whether he could feel the gun in her pants.

"I missed you." Black breathed the words into her mouth. He placed her onto the bed. They were both out of breath. The tornado-eye of different emotions whipping around them included love, lust, hurt, betrayal, and revenge. It was a deadly mix.

"Fuck," she panted excitedly. She inched back and slipped her gun under one pillow. "I want you," Donna panted.

Black breathed out excitedly.

Suddenly, a memory of their first time swirled into Donna's mind. She remembered how good it felt. How loved she had felt. She remembered thinking she never wanted to be away from him ever in life.

"I want you too. I always wanted you. I always fucking loved you," Black wheezed hungrily, anticipation of what was coming taking his breath away.

Donna looked up with lustful eyes at his beautiful, shiny dark skin and the layers of muscle that made up his abdomen, and she felt her insides grind with wanting. Wasting no more time, she swiftly got out of her clothes to reveal her body. The adrenaline coursing through her body didn't allow her to think about how and what was next.

"Let me ride it like old times," Donna whispered in a low growl as she climbed on top of Black.

Their skin burned against one another, the heat threatening to set the entire room on fire.

"Yeah, that's what I'm talking about," he gasped.

"Don't move. Let me do the work," Donna warned, straddling him. She felt his erect dick pressing on her clit, and she was ready to explode.

Black moved so that he could enter her.

"Let me do it," Donna corrected.

Black relented and went still.

Donna lifted her hips and drove her pelvis down onto him. "Ah," she belted out in ecstasy.

Black followed with a bellow of his own. Before long, their bodies were moving in sync.

"Black! Are you here?" A shrill female voice cut through the air and brought Donna crashing back to reality.

"Fuck!" Black huffed. He tried to move, but Donna quickly slipped her hand under the pillow for her gun.

"Black? Where the fuck you at?" the female called out. This time, her voice was closer.

"Don't fucking move," Donna gritted through her teeth.

Black's eyes bulged. He knew how this would play out. He shifted uncomfortably, but Donna pressed her weight down on him.

The banging on the door came with a fury. Donna wouldn't even turn her head, because she knew he would buck her off of him, and it would leave her fucked up.

"Black, you motherfucker!" she growled from behind them.

That was Donna's signal. "This is for robbing me and leaving me for dead."

With the swift movement of a trained professional, she let off two shots into Black's head, then turned, and shot the girl center mass in the chest.

"Oh, shit!" the girl squawked.

Donna looked back into Black's face, and his eyes were open with shock. "You never loved me," she said, climbing off the bed.

"Ahh!" the girl gagged, her hands instinctively grabbing at her chest.

Donna stood over her as her body bucked wildly, fighting for air. "Guess you were at the wrong place at the wrong time," she said. With that, she pumped two more bullets into the girl.

Donna looked around and back at Black, his face covered in blood. Sadness trampled through her. She thought she'd feel a sense of accomplishment, but she didn't. Just pure sadness.

"You left me no choice," Donna gritted as she went to work making sure she didn't leave any traces of herself behind. Now it was time to find Kim, so they could get on with their lives.

"No more running. We will find these motherfuckers and finish them all," Donna promised as she left the scene of the crime.

Chapter 12

Donna's head throbbed with pain from lack of sleep, hunger, and just plain stress. After her deadly reunion with Black, she jumped in the car and just drove without stopping. She cried hard as she drove. Donna loved Black. He was her first and only love. She would never be the same.

Donna blinked rapidly, trying to correct her vision as it started to blur. Her heart jumped when she read a sign: WELCOME TO LOUISIANA. Donna cracked a dry, halfhearted smile; all that she could manage once she realized she'd finally made it. She'd see her sister very soon, so long as no more wrenches got thrown into her plans.

It seemed like she had been driving for a hundred years. She'd already heard on the news radio station that Black's house had been turned into the scene of a double homicide investigation. The news reporters had called the crimes "heinous" and "cold-blooded."

Murder wasn't her style, but she'd learned that sometimes you had to do what you had to do. It was survival of the fittest in her mind. Do or die. All she could think of was getting to Kim and getting out of the country. It was clear now that they weren't going to be safe in any state in the U.S. Everywhere Donna had turned, there was someone after them.

Being in Louisiana, Donna was so close to Kim she could really feel it in her body—the excitement of the escape. She could actually visualize Kim rushing to her with tears, hugs, and cheers of victory and relief. Donna still didn't know if Kim had made it yet, but she was praying that she had. Thoughts of reuniting with Kim were constantly running through her mind.

As Donna pulled toward a small gas station, she turned up the radio just to make sure she was still good and that the manhunt in Texas hadn't landed itself near where she was. Donna parked and went inside the convenience store connected to the gas station. She wanted to freshen up, take a breather. She was sure to pull the hat she had stolen from Black's house down low over her eyes and close the oversized jacket, too. She had Black's girlfriend's ID in her wallet just in case. It might've been stupid to have a dead bitch's ID, but Donna knew if she got pulled over, she couldn't use her own.

Donna went inside, ordered her gas, and headed to the bathroom. She splashed water on her face and decided, after looking at herself in the scratched-up mirror, that she looked horrible. Everything had taken a real toll on her. She realized now how much of a charmed life she and Kim had been living with Aunt Lisa, doing licks, having money to burn just because they hadn't really worked for it, and living a lavish life. Donna shook her head at how it all had changed so fast. Now she literally looked like a homeless person.

"Not for long. Get to Kim, get the fuck out of dodge, and live to see another day," she whispered to herself.

Once she relieved herself and got her scrambled thoughts together, she left the bathroom. As she made her way back into the store, her steps were halted by the sound of voices. Donna stepped back, stood against the wall, and listened.

"Have you heard about these sisters going on a killing spree? They killed their auntie, then five men are dead, and police in Texas think it's them. Another poor girl got killed, too."

"Well, I bet-not see either one of them, because I'll be sure turning them in for the reward," the store clerk said, followed by a hearty laugh.

"Yeah, that reward is pretty big now. But they probably out of town by now and heading who knows where," the customer said.

"Well, you know they described the car they think they might be driving, too, so I gotta be on the lookout. You know what I mean?" The clerk chuckled again.

"Please, they ain't coming nowhere close to this place. So, I guess we both outta luck on that reward." The customer grabbed her bag off the counter and smiled at the clerk. "I'll see you tomorrow."

Donna swallowed hard and shook her head. Her heart was beating so painfully fast that she lost her breath. She doubled back toward the bathroom to check her disguise and make sure she was unrecognizable. There was no way she was even going to chance taking the car. Now she had no transportation.

Back in the bathroom, her body was wet with nervous sweat. With labored breaths, she snatched the hat off. She took her hair and worked hard to make sure it was all stuffed under the hat. Donna removed the jacket and dumped it into the trashcan, leaving her in just a T-shirt.

Loud pounding on the door almost gave her a heart attack. She jumped so fast urine came out of her bladder.

"Someone is in here!" Donna yelled. Then she heard what sounded like a small commotion outside the door. Her mind started racing. She imagined a swarm of police outside the door, guns drawn, waiting for her. Donna paced and bit her bottom lip hard, trying to figure out what to do next. Her legs got weak when she thought about her limited options. She pictured Kim being all alone in the world, and that gave her some motivation.

"You're going to get out of this, Donna. You will get to your sister, and all will be good," she pep-talked herself.

"Only God can get me out of this," Donna whispered. As a child, she had lost faith in God. Donna never understood what kind of God would take a child's parents away from them. Now she needed a miracle.

A cold feeling took over her body. Her lips began to tremble, and her teeth began to chatter. "They about to come in here and get your ass," she said with finality. "This is the end, Donna," she said in a low murmur.

With that, she rushed to the bathroom door, unlocked it, and opened it. She was ready to be on the defensive, since she'd decided she wasn't going out without a fight. Donna's eyes went wide, and her jaw went slack, but then her shoulders slumped with relief.

Standing outside the door was a mother bouncing a round-faced baby boy on her hip. The young woman cracked a partial smile at Donna and nodded toward the bathroom.

"Didn't mean to rush, but we got one of those up-the-back poops going on," the mother said, crinkling up her nose like she was disgusted.

Donna nodded and glanced at the men's bathroom. It had a window inside. Her heart sped up again. As the other woman went into the women's room, Donna looked up and down the small hallway at the back of the store to make sure no one was coming. She listened for a few seconds, and she could hear police sirens. Someone must have spotted her car and called the police. In fact, is sounded like a lot of police officers were there now.

Donna rushed into the men's bathroom and locked the door behind her. She had just gotten a second chance. She wasn't ready to give up after all.

"That was either you, God, or Aunt Lisa is looking out for me," Donna whispered to herself. She climbed on the sink under the window and hoisted herself up. The first time she tried, she slipped back down.

"Damn!" she huffed. She inhaled and exhaled and tried it again. This time, she was able to get up on the window-sill. Donna had a hard time, but with some twisting of her torso, she finally squeezed through the window and tumbled onto the gravel outside. When she hit the rocky ground, she had the wind knocked out of her. Dazed for a moment, she pulled it together.

She scrambled to her feet and took off running into the woods behind the store. With no car and no way to get to her meet-up with Kim, Donna walked in what she assumed was the correct direction. She planned to keep walking until she found her way back to her sister. She had no other choice.

After almost six hours of walking, Donna's feet were swollen, and her back felt like someone had hit her with a bag of bricks. She knew she needed a rest, or she would pass out and probably be found by the police.

While walking through the woods, she was able to see the road and a few stores and scattered restaurants. Donna knew she needed to rest, and it was risky to go out into the open without knowing how close the police were. She opted to finally stop at a small, hole-in-the-wall spot at the side of the road. Her mind was muddled with thoughts of a being back in her luxury house, in her warm bed, laughing with Kim and listening to Aunt Lisa tell them stories of her partying days.

Donna had been thinking about Black a lot. She still couldn't shake how things had turned out. She also couldn't shake the deep feelings that kept popping into her mind for him, even after what he had done. Donna kept imag-ining how life would've been had she been able to settle down with him, become his wife, and have his kids back in the day. She had definitely chosen the fast life over that life. It was a fantasy for her to believe she could ever have a regular love life, especially now. It made her sad to realize how much she and Kim had given up, even as a young girl. Donna promised herself never to fall in love again if it hurt this badly.

Once Donna climbed the six steps up to the restaurant door, she stumbled to a table. She was so tired that she could barely move into the booth without feeling like it was a chore.

Donna couldn't keep her head up another minute. She put her head down on her arms and finally let out a long, cleansing sigh. If she didn't run the risk of too much attention, she would've cried. But now wasn't the time to get weak. As usual, she had to stay strong, bite her feelings, and keep on trucking.

Donna believed there was no way her parents would've wanted this life for her and Kim. What had happened to them all? It was like one day, they all had everything, and the next, it was all gone. One minute, Donna and Kim were riding high, living a life most people their ages only dreamed of—traveling, shopping, partying and wanting for nothing. Within the blink of an eye—or the spark of a gun—everything had been snatched away. Someone wanted to see them suffer, and they weren't going to give up until it was a reality.

The more Donna thought about it, the more she figured that it had to be someone close to them. No one else would've known about Aunt Lisa's burial and funeral services. It had definitely crossed her mind that Keraun might've turned on them, but each time the thought even popped into her head, Donna would shake it off. Nah, not Keraun. He was Aunt Lisa's best friend. He was Kim's lover. Besides, he'd helped them with every lick, and he was like family. Donna didn't want to even consider that those closest to you might one day grow jealous of you. No matter how hard she tried to deny it, it was still embedded deep in her mind that he may have had something to do with Aunt Lisa's death. After all, she did shoot his ass.

Being on the run with no real place to go and no way to contact her sister wasn't exactly what Donna had envisioned for either of them. She hadn't really ever envisioned any hard times while she was growing up being lavished with the finest things. Donna never thought further than their next lick, but she did always fantasize about living a normal life where they didn't have to steal and she could be with Black. Donna had to wonder if this fate that she and Kim were suffering now was karma finally catching up to them. She also had to wonder about just how much she had really given up for the life she had lived.

The waitress finally came to Donna's table. The place wasn't really crowded, and only a few booths were occupied. Donna ordered some food two cups of coffee. She needed the caffeine to stay awake. She also needed energy, so she could run out on the bill. Her bag had been in the car left at the gas station. All she had on her was the $10 she'd taken into the store to grab snacks.

As Donna waited, she noticed a small television hanging behind the counter in a corner. The sound was muted, but she saw her and Kim's name streaming along the bottom of the screen. They were pegging them as the most wanted women in the South in fifteen years.

Donna pulled her hat lower and kept her head down so that the restaurant staff wouldn't recognize her before she drank her coffee and rested up for the next leg of her journey. She planned to scarf down the food and hit the road before too many people came into the nearly empty place.

Suddenly, Donna noticed someone approaching her table in her peripheral vision. She clenched her fists and got on the defensive. *Be ready for anything. Be ready for anything. Trust no one. Be ready for anything,* Donna chanted in her head as she realized it was a dude approaching.

"You always eat by yourself?" he said.

Donna let out a long sigh. She was in no mood for the bullshit. First of all, if he was picking up women in this hole-in-the-wall, he couldn't be about shit. Donna turned her head slowly, wearing a scowl on her face. She was almost blinded by the heavy diamond-encrusted chains hanging around the man's thick neck. Something dinged in Donna's mind—a lick! Money was what she needed to get the rest of the way on her journey. She immediately started casing the dude as a lick. It was a habit. She was so used to making dudes out to be victims in her mind as soon as she met them that it happened almost automatically now. Donna's eyes darted around, trying to see who he might be there with.

"You always interrupt people when they're eating?" Donna replied with attitude.

Her attitude didn't faze the dude one bit. "Naw, I only interrupt beautiful women sitting all alone in the middle of my hood," the man said with a Southern drawl. "I'm Butchy," he said, extending his hand.

Donna raised a brow, unimpressed, but she extended her hand in response to his dangling hand nonetheless. She had money and getting to Kim on her mind. Period.

"Angie," Donna said, giving a fake name as she shook Butchy's hand. She quickly noticed that he also had huge rings on each of his fingers on both hands. Some were gold, some were filled with diamonds, and some were black, which Donna took as onyx. That was a new thing in the South—niggas were wearing onyx and other gemstone jewelry. Butchy looked like the typical country drug dealer. He also looked kind of corny, like he'd make the perfect lick, so Donna's interest was definitely piqued.

It didn't take but a minute for Donna to determine that Butchy was the type of nigga she and Kim would usually make light work out of setting up and turning into one of their paydays. Butchy was flashy, which meant he most likely wore everything he had to his name. Donna had seen it many times before—the typical hood attention-whore dude who wanted everybody to notice him. Usually the real out-there ones like that were the easiest to set up for the downfall.

All of a sudden, Donna's day didn't seem to be going too bad after all. In fact, she had a newfound energy to press on. The one thing she never doubted on this rough journey was her ability to survive. Her skills were top notch, and now her mind was in motion with thoughts of getting her hands on a car so she could make it the rest of the way.

Donna knew she had to play hard to get with Butchy and do the things she and Kim had mastered over the years. Aunt Lisa had preached so much that Donna could probably recite all the jewels of knowledge in her sleep. The most important one when setting up a lick was to remember that being too eager was a sure way to run a shallow nigga away, because those look-at-me-now dudes always wanted a challenge. Men like that loved the thrill of the chase. Donna wanted to snag Butchy, but she also had to be careful about being recognized.

"So, what's up, Angie? You want to hang out, let me get to know you?" Butchy asked, partly a sly grin. "Show you how we do it down in the land of the saints."

"Nah. I'm not in town for that long. Sorry," Donna answered just as her food arrived. She turned toward her plate as if she was totally uninterested in him or whatever he had to say.

"At least let a nigga buy your food then," Butchy said, slapping a hundred-dollar bill down on her table. He smiled at Donna, so she knew he was showing off. But that didn't change the fact that she'd noticed him peel the hundred off a pretty thick stack of bills from his pocket—a stack she needed to get her hands on.

Donna rolled her eyes and chuckled at his hundred-dollar bill shenanigans. She wasn't about to let him make her the cheap trick.

"What makes you think I need you to pick up my tab?" Donna asked sassily. She knew damn well she was elated to see that money. Now she wouldn't have to dine and dash.

Since Butchy had wanted her to notice everything he had, she obliged and started taking mental inventory. The thief in her was saying Butchy was an easy lick, but she'd have to spend some time and get him to let his guards down. The logical person inside of her was saying there was no way she could risk him recognizing her, so she'd have to settle for that hundred dollars and call it a day.

"I didn't say you needed it. Just felt like it was the gentlemanly thing to do," Butchy said.

"Something inside of me is saying there ain't much gentlemanly about you," Donna said. "But thanks, though. Today must be your lucky day. I'll let you pay for my coffee and act like you're a gentleman," Donna said, playing it off when really she was so fucking relieved he'd paid her bill.

Butchy looked amused. He'd fallen for trap number one with her. Donna knew shit like that always made men go even harder to get a girl. It was a proven formula that Aunt Lisa had taught her and Kim. They'd used it hundreds of times, and it worked the same every time.

"Sassy and beautiful . . . I like that," he said, winking at Donna.

"You like that? You sure? Seems like you don't get many sassy chicks talking back. I bet they be falling down at your feet," Donna said, chuckling. Butchy was like a game to her now. He wasn't handsome, but he also wasn't what she considered ugly. He was dressed nice, and everything he wore was obligatorily expensive. Typical.

"Naw. You got me fucked up. That ain't never been me. Naw, baby girl, I like ladies," Butchy replied. As soon as the nickname floated out of his mouth, Donna sat up straight. There was something about the slick way he said the nickname Keraun had used for her and Kim over the years that made Donna uneasy. Maybe that was a sign from God? She needed to dismiss him, eat, and keep it trucking on out of there.

Donna was exhausted anyway. Without Kim and without knowing Aunt Lisa and Keraun were somewhere with her back, Donna didn't know if it was smart to pull off a lick alone. If Butchy wasn't going to serve the purpose she needed, which was a car and some money, she couldn't afford to waste any more precious time. She gulped her second cup of coffee, and without much of a goodbye, she headed out of the restaurant without even acknowledging him after he went back to say something to his friends.

Butchy followed Donna with his eyes and nodded his head. She had a gut feeling this nigga wasn't going to give up so easily. She just wanted to get far away before he realized she was as desperate as she really was.

Donna hadn't even made it half a mile down the road on foot before she heard that familiar drawl.

"C'mon, Angie, now. Look atcha. Tell me why a beautiful girl like you out here on these mean country roads on your pretty feet," Butchy called out to her from his Benz truck.

Not another bad-luck Benz truck, Donna thought to herself. She stopped and turned toward his car as he inched it along beside her.

"I gotta tell you, you are one persistent motherfucker," Donna said, shaking her head.

Butchy laughed at her, still amused by her fiery attitude. It wasn't lost on him that she was beautiful, but she definitely looked like she was down on her luck. Butchy had been around; Donna could tell that too. He probably knew a chick in distress when he saw one. She knew he could tell she was hiding some pain and running from something. She also knew niggas like him loved to take advantage of girls like her.

"Why don't you let me give you a ride to wherever? I swear, I'm not a serial killer. I'm just a cool dude trying to get to know a spitfire girl. You can't walk but so far on this road, and you damn sure can't walk on that freeway," Butchy yelled.

Donna's head was kind of spinning from the pain in her throbbing feet and aching legs, but she was damn sure not going to let him know she was that desperate.

"Let me give you a ride to wherever you're going, Angie," Butchy continued. "You got my word. This is about helping you . . . nothing else. Swear 'fore God. Plus, I'm already scared of you and that mouth. And look, I left all my boys in the restaurant just so I could chase you down. That gotta say something," he said, pressing his point home.

Donna stopped walking, rolled her eyes, and turned toward his truck. She tilted her head and stared at Butchy for a second to see if he'd recognize her at all from the news. He smiled like a Cheshire cat, and she almost had to put her arm up because all of his chains were blinding her. If he did recognize her, she wasn't able to tell. Because, what kind of street dude would pick up a bitch that was most wanted? Not many.

After some thought, Donna convinced herself that Butchy was clearly a street dude that didn't look or sound like he watched the news, and he damn sure didn't act like he recognized her as a fugitive. He was definitely a drug dealer; that much she had already figured out, so maybe this was a sign from God that he was the ride that she needed. Maybe Butchy was her sure way to Kim.

"You coming?" he asked, still smiling. "I can't sit in the middle of the road like this. Too much attention."

Donna's shoulders eased a bit as she resigned herself to Butchy being her only choice. "I'm coming, but if you try anything, you are going to feel a wrath you don't want to fuck with," Donna threatened in a dead serious tone. She didn't have her gun on her, but she certainly had lifted a small steak knife from the restaurant. If she hadn't learned how to kill a man by knife before, she would sure learn today if this nigga tried anything funny.

"Man, just get in the car. You already know I ain't trying nothing funny," Butchy said snidely.

Once Donna climbed up into the truck, she relaxed against the seat. The butter-soft leather cushions felt so damn good to her sore muscles. This was how she was supposed to be living, not running from some unknown enemy and the police. Donna sighed with relief in her mind. There was no way she could've walked another mile.

Donna was laughing and joking with Butchy before she even knew it. She had let her guard down, but not all the way. She wanted him to think she was at ease, but never that. Donna was smarter than that. She had to admit that Butchy was amusing, and he was almost like a comedian. Donna didn't know if it was his accent or just his wit, but she found him to be hilarious and genuinely a nice dude. He talked about everything from what he called dumb-ass drug dealers, ratchet-ass cops, and his many baby mamas. Donna felt like she was at a comedy show. That's how hard she was rolling with laughter from Butchy's stories.

"Gurrrl, you think I'm joking? These country-ass baby mamas send a nigga to the po' house. They be calling me like, 'Butchy, I'ma need some toilet paper t'day. Ya baby gotta wipe his ass.' I'm like, 'Bitch, you called me yest'day and asked fo' Pampers. Now, which one is it?'" Butchy joked.

Donna cackled. "Well, you picked them, right?"

"Maaaan, listen. A nigga like me dumb as fuck. Shit, I took longer to pick out dis outfit than I did picking bitches to have my kids with. They all off the chain," Butchy said, shaking his head and laughing at the same time.

Donna laughed at him too. "So, you telling me out of all them baby mamas, you ain't never love a single one of them?" she asked through her laughs.

"There was one I loved, but she broke my heart. I got locked up, and when I came home to nothing, she was gone. Next man had her," Butchy continued, getting a bit more serious. "Ain't no feeling like that in the world. When you locked up, you be looking forward to what you got on the outside, so to come home and it's gone . . . nigga liable to lose his mind."

Donna fell silent for a few seconds. She felt like Black was talking to her from the grave. She felt the pain behind Butchy's words, and for the first time, she really understood the impact her actions had on Black.

"What about you? In love? Ever been in love? Kids?" Butchy shot questions at her.

Donna was kind of stuck on stupid, the way she got anytime she thought about Black. "Naw. I am trying too hard to figure life out for all of that," she replied, her voice trailing off as she turned to look out the window.

"I hear that," Butchy said. He seemed to notice the shift in her mood, but he didn't quit with his questions. He started asking her where she was from and things about her family life.

Donna was usually good at making up shit on the fly, but she really just wanted to be silent. She was honest with Butchy about having to meet up with Kim in New Orleans, though. She figured maybe it would speed up the process of getting there. Donna told him her sister already lived there and needed her.

Butchy listened to her, but he kept peeking at her out of the corner of his eye like he didn't fully believe her. A blind man could see that Donna wasn't on a normal trek to New Orleans. She looked like she had been through hell; she had no car, seemingly no money. Something wasn't adding up for him, but he was going to play it off like he was just happy to be in her company. It still amazed him how easily and fluidly some women told bold-faced lies, though. What Donna didn't know was that two could play that game.

As Butchy and Donna drove closer to her destination, Donna's insides were churning with anticipation about getting there. Although she hadn't figured out exactly how she would get rid of him, she was still overjoyed. She was doing a victory dance in her head, because she felt like she'd won the battle against a bunch of very dangerous killers that were hunting for her. Donna had evaded death as if she had an angel riding with her everywhere she went. Donna could hear Aunt Lisa and her father in her head, telling her how proud they were of her making it this far all alone. She smiled just thinking about them. She missed the fuck out of all of them.

"A'ight, Angie, we almost there," Butchy announced, noticing that Donna had started fading out on him. "I gotta make a quick pit stop, if you know what I mean," he said, holding his crotch for emphasis.

Donna wanted to tell him hell no, no stopping! But she couldn't do that. He had done her a huge favor. She was not in a position to argue. Her stomach cramped up. She liked him, but she didn't ever trust anyone fully.

Butchy pulled into a rest stop and threw his truck into park. "This ain't no joke!" he exclaimed, rushing out of the truck and running into the rest stop bathroom.

Donna was alone, in a luxury vehicle, with the keys running. Her heart throttled up. She liked Butchy, but damn, how could she pass up this opportunity? Thoughts swirled around in her head. She looked around the rest stop parking lot and contemplated stealing the truck and leaving Butchy behind. That way, she could drive herself all the way before the full stolen car report would be out.

"Fuck, fuck, fuck," Donna chanted, biting her nails furiously. In any other case, she would've treated Butchy like any other lick and left his ass for dead. But now, she was torn, because Butchy had turned out to be such a nice guy. Leaving him stranded would be grimy, but grimy was also what it was going to take for her to get where she was going. Besides, there was nothing more grimy than everything that had ever happened in her life.

Donna looked down and noticed that Butchy had left his phone behind in the cup holder between the seats. He must've really had to piss. She saw his screen flashing with messages. Figuring it was one of the funny-ass baby mamas, Donna picked up the phone and read the text messages that were coming through. Donna's eyes went round, and her mouth fell open. She was holding her breath and didn't even realize it as she scanned the messages.

"Oh my God! You have got to be fucking kidding me!" Donna wolfed out the words as she read two text messages that had her name in it and an old picture of her. Donna clasped her hand over her mouth, because she felt like throwing up.

Who the fuck does Butchy know that knows me? He knew me all along?

From the texts, Donna learned that whoever Butchy was working for was the same person that was after her—and the person wanted to put hands on her before the police did.

This slick country bastard set me the fuck up!

Donna could've jumped in the driver's seat and peeled out. In fact, that was what she should've done; but Donna decided that Butchy had to die. Revenge. If not for anything else, he had to die for luring her in like an animal to slaughter. Thinking quickly, Donna jumped out of the passenger's seat and slid into the back of the truck. She was smart enough to know that there was no way she could confront Butchy head on. He clearly weighed over 225 pounds, and more than likely was strapped.

Donna had devised a plan. She just had to pray to God it worked. The adrenaline coursing through her had made the body fatigue fade away. Donna was in flight or fight mode, and she had decided to fucking fight.

Butchy returned to the car and looked around strangely, trying to figure out where the hell his cute little car companion had gone.

"Where the fuck this girl done gone? I ain't got time for the bullshit," Butchy mumbled under his breath.

Donna's insides were roiling with anger so hard she felt like she'd taken drugs. She could barely keep still, but patience was essential, and she knew it. She waited a few minutes. Before she could move in for the kill, Butchy picked up his phone. Donna fell back so she could hear his conversation first.

"Let me holla at the boss," Butchy grumbled into his phone.

Donna was about to get up, but she wanted to hear everything first. She bit down into her lip so hard that she drew her own blood. Donna could feel the heat of anger coursing through her veins. She was more mad at herself than anyone. How could she have been so fucking stupid?

"Aye, boss. I got the package. Yeah, I been picked up on her. You said she might be going to New York. . . . Naw, the bitch said she going to see her sick sister in New Orleans. I know you said you wanted her alive. That's the only reason I ain't did shit to her yet. I'm good with blowing her fucking brains out for a extra ten Gs, ya dig. . . . A'ight, calm down, nigga. I will deliver her in one piece so you can do what you want with her. Alls I need is for you to have my money right. I mean, she cute and all, but you know a nigga like me ain't got no love for a bitch. We gon' do an even exchange—my money for this bitch's life. Don't play no slick shit on me, ya heard," Butchy said. He was speaking like a totally different person. Donna didn't even recognize the voice he was using or anything. He hung up.

"Where is this bitch?" Butchy huffed.

Donna was about to burst inside. She was beyond hot with anger now as she listened to Butchy call her all sorts of bitches and say he could kill her on the spot. Her mind raced in a million different directions, but one thing that was clear to her was that Butchy had to die.

Donna hated the feeling of betrayal. It was very reminiscent of what she felt about Black, so that alone was fueling the fire burning inside of her even more.

"A'ight, this bitch taking too long. I'ma have to get out and lay my pimp hand down on a bitch," Butchy said, laughing to himself.

Donna had heard enough. She sucked in her bottom lip and balled her fists so tightly her knuckles ached. It was time. She slowly rose up from behind him like a ghost. Butchy caught a quick glimpse of her in his rearview mirror, and he almost jumped out of his skin.

"What the fuck—" Butchy started when he noticed Donna behind, but his words were cut short.

"You piece of shit!" Donna used her forearm and locked it around his neck from the back. She grabbed Butchy in a tight chokehold and placed her stolen steak knife to his face.

"You fucking lying piece of shit," Donna gritted, squeezing as hard as she could. "You tried to set me up? You don't know who the fuck I am," she hissed in his ear.

"I . . . I don't know whatchu—Wha . . . what . . . whatchu doin'?" Butchy gurgled as Donna used the limited strength she had left in her body to choke off his air supply. Her arm ached as she pulled it. She had him in such a position of disadvantage now. One false move and that knife would've plunged right into his jugular.

"Who is your boss? And what do they want with me?" Donna hissed in Butchy's ear, jamming the sharp tip of the knife hard into his temple.

Butchy gurgled and spit, trying to get air. He couldn't believe Donna was that strong being that she was so small in stature.

"Who the fuck is it?" Donna growled, swiping the knife over his cheek until she drew blood.

Butchy gurgled as blood leaked from his cheek. Donna didn't even care if people could see through His dark tints. At that point, she had nothing to lose.

"I . . . don't . . . I don't," Butchy garbled out.

Donna cut him again, just because she couldn't believe what he was saying. Butchy was shaking as he started to lose air.

"I know you know what they want. But you know what? you want to die for some motherfucker that could care less about you, then fuck it. Fuck you and fuck your fake-ass boss," Donna hissed with finality.

"Mmmm," Butchy moaned. There was no mercy for him in her eyes.

Donna moved her arm just enough to stick the knife in the right spot and drag it across his neck. Butchy fell forward, holding his throat, but Donna knew it would only be a matter of seconds.

Donna got her bearings and scrambled for the door. She wasn't even spooked anymore. It was all or nothing at this point.

Donna rushed around the outside of the vehicle, mustered up enough strength, and pulled Butchy's body out of the driver's seat and let him fall on the ground. "Bastard-ass traitor," she grumbled. With that, she jumped into Butchy's driver's seat, reversed out of the rest area like a madwoman, and with screeching tires, she peeled onto the highway toward her destination. Donna knew it would only be a matter of minutes before the rest area would be swarming with police and crime scene vehicles. Again, she had dodged a very close call.

"Thank you, Aunt Lisa," she murmured. Donna was convinced now that there was an angel riding with her, and she was going to make it to reunite with her sister after all.

Chapter 13

Kim drove the car into New Orleans and felt like a million tons of stress had been lifted from her shoulders. She'd dodged so many roadblocks on her way. The murders were still weighing on her mind. Kim knew that time was definitely running out.

She parked in a hotel parking lot adjacent to Bourbon Street and let out a long, exasperated breath. Kim could see the spot Aunt Lisa had planned out for them up ahead, so she exited the car. Her body was tingling all over, and her insides felt like they were jumping around. She couldn't wait to see her sister. They'd had their differences of opinions sometimes, but damn if Kim didn't miss the shit out of Donna.

She saw crowds of people bustling through the busy streets of downtown New Orleans. "Good. I'll blend right in. Hopefully Donna got the stash and we can get the fuck out of here," Kim mumbled. She would just blend into the crowd and pray she didn't stick out in any way.

Kim kept her head down as she ambled forward to the spot. When she stood in front of it, her heart almost exploded out of her chest.

Oh my God! I fucking made it! she screamed inside of her head. Kim wanted so badly to dance and sing, but she knew better than that. That would be undue attention at a time when she was so damn close.

Tears streamed down her face like a waterfall, and she stood on weak, wobbly legs. Even the stink of Bourbon

Street stench smelled like heaven in that moment. Kim swiped at the tears on her face and told herself she had to pull it together. Her journey wasn't one hundred percent complete just yet. She had finally made it, but now she had to pray Donna would be there soon.

Kim didn't even know if Donna was still alive. The thought that her sister might never show up almost doubled her over with nausea.

Think positive, she told herself. *Donna is going to show up, and everything is going to be all right.* For the first time since this entire ordeal began, Kim was able to let out a deep sigh of relief. Her feelings of relief were short-lived. There was some commotion, and a bunch of cops began swarming the streets.

Fuck! Kim cursed to herself. It was too risky to stay there. She rushed away from the scene and ducked into a small boutique hotel. It was cute, but she knew it would be expensive. Kim was so exhausted that she could practically taste sleep. Her stomach growled. Everything was going wrong. And where the fuck was Donna?

Kim took the last of the money from Keraun and got a room. She would have to wait out the commotion and then go check to back for her sister. Once she got into the hotel room, she didn't waste any time stripping and racing to the shower.

"Oh my God! This water feels so good." She whirled around under the hot stream of water. Kim told herself she'd never take simple things for granted again. Who would've thought something as simple as a hot shower could feel like a million dollars to her? Kim realized being raised to not really have to work for anything and living the high life had made her spoiled and ungrateful. She'd taken a lot of shit for granted, ignoring the possibility that karma would catch up to her eventually. It was going to be a new start for her and Donna. Kim wasn't going to let them suffer, but she was also not going to do grimy shit to people anymore either.

After her shower, Kim jumped straight into the bed. The bed felt like a small bit of heaven. Before she knew it, a deep sleep overcame her, and so did dreams of the past and of her family. . . .

"Here's to life and us and the world that is ours," Aunt Lisa said as she toasted with Keraun, Kim, and Donna. The toast signaled the end of a long lick they had pulled off and the big payday that followed.

Donna and Kim were smiling. Under Aunt Lisa's tutelage, Kim and Donna had pulled off a well-played lick that took a lot of work. The fruits of their labor—stacks of cash—sat at their feet in duffle bags. They all raised their glasses to join in the toast. Aunt Lisa finally smiled. That had never been an easy feat either. Kim and Donna's chests swelled with pride. They loved nothing more than making Aunt Lisa proud.

As they drank champagne and celebrated, Kim was already talking about their next lick.

"Just chill and enjoy this," Donna had told her. "We don't ever live in the moment. We are always on to the next biggest thing. Life sometimes has to be about living in the moment."

"Okay, okay, old lady. Damn. Let a bitch live," Kim relented with a laugh.

Aunt Lisa shook her head at them. Kim could see the love in Aunt Lisa's eyes, even though she was sometimes super hard on them.

"We ain't gonna talk about new licks, but we also gonna make sure we stay on our Ps and Qs like usual. Just because we came through on the other side of this one doesn't mean there might not still be some blow back," Aunt Lisa said seriously.

Keraun nodded his head in agreement. "Yo, I gotta bounce up out of here. Y'all did good," Keraun said as he picked his bag of money.

Kim watched him with love in her eyes. They owed a lot to Keraun. He had put them up on all the licks, and he held them down when everything was going down with them. He was also their security and mentor out there, since he had a lot of street connections. Just a totally standup guy in their eyes.

"Damn, you that's all the celebrating you about to do?" Aunt Lisa asked, trying to mask the disappointment in her voice.

Kim felt like she could always feel something between Aunt Lisa and Keraun. Too bad Keraun had already begun seducing her at that point. Aunt Lisa couldn't have him.

"Naw, it's not like that. I just got a lot of shit out here to take care of."

Keraun walked toward the door but stopped before he went through it and winked at them.

"I can go with you," Aunt Lisa said. Now the desperation was obvious.

Kim and Donna looked at one another strangely.

"Nah, I'm good. Stay here and celebrate with your nieces. They deserve it, and so do you. Y'all deserve everything y'all get. Save me some of that champagne, though," Keraun said, and with that, he headed out the back door.

"Bye, Big K," Kim called after him.

Not even ten minutes later . . .

BANG! BOOM! *The door came crashing in!*

Kim was jerked out of her dream, which ended more like a nightmare. "Mmfh!" She tried to scream, but a leather glove clamped down forcefully over her nose and mouth. She couldn't breathe, and her eyes were stretched so wide they hurt at the edges.

Not again!

Kim kicked her legs and tried to flail her arms, but she was no match for the men that had their hands all over her. Her heart threatened to bust from her chest, and urine escaped her bladder.

"I must admit, you were good up until now. It took a lot to find you. You're pretty fucking smart," a man hissed as his helpers bound and gagged Kim. "Everything you've done has come back to haunt you. That bitch karma, she always finds you," the man said in an eerie voice.

"Tie this bitch up!" he commanded, unleashing his goons on her like wild dogs on a piece of meat. "We got a very important family reunion to attend."

They began raining punches down all over Kim's body at will because she just wouldn't stop fighting. The pain that engulfed her entire body was like nothing she'd ever felt before.

How did they find me? Why? She was screaming in her head. She opened her mouth to scream, but a gag was immediately stuffed in it, so her efforts were for nothing. They taunted her as they beat her, hitting her like she was a man. A punch to her left temple sent little squirms of light flitting through her eyes and threatened to make her black out.

Pain was clouding her mind as someone dragged her onto the floor. Her back and tailbone crashed against the floor, sending a shockwave of pain straight up her spine. Suddenly, her legs went completely numb. Before they placed the ropes around her feet, one of the men let out a loud, maniacal cackle and then kicked her in the stomach. Kim was forced over onto her stomach, and her arms were wrenched behind her back until her shoulders locked. Next, one of the men stomped on her back, and she felt something inside crack and pop. They hog-tied her hands so tight around the wrist that her fingers went completely numb. She was hoisted up and hit at least a hundred more times before they finally decided it was time to move her. A black bag was placed over her head as they dragged her from her hotel room.

Kim could feel dirt and gravel from the ground embedding itself in her delicate skin. If this beating was anything like the death they were going to subject her to, she wished for it to happen immediately. She thought about how Donna would react when she found out Kim was dead. An eruption of vomit spewed up from Kim's stomach and threatened to choke her to death.

Tears streamed down her face in buckets. She had made it to the spot and was so close to reuniting with Donna, but now, she was probably going to die at the hands of these strangers and never see her sister again.

Bound, gagged, brutally beaten, and barely clinging to consciousness, Kim was finally thrown into the back of a van. She was a mess of blood, vomit, and urine. She knew she was dying, because she had heard older people always say all of your bodily fluids release right before you die. Kim had blacked out and come back into consciousness a few times since the beating had started. Her body involuntarily curled in on itself until she lay in a tight fetal position. Flashes of Donna and Aunt Lisa and even her parents flitted through Kim's mind. She was slipping. Life was slipping.

Kim could hear muddled voices, but nothing was clear. The pain shooting through the base of her skull was probably a signal of a fractured skull as well. She felt like every single one of her ribs was broken, and she found it hard to take even a small breath without a ball of pain exploding through her torso.

She could smell the strong scent of men's cologne, weed smoke, and gunpowder all around her. After a while, it seemed to her like the movement of the van got slower. Although her eyes were covered, she could sense the presence of a lot of people in the van with her, maybe more than just the ones that had snatched her. Kim had no fight left in her. She had finally been defeated by her journey to get away from Houston and meet up with her sister.

It felt like she had been riding for days when the van finally came to a complete stop. The hushed tones of the attackers discussing her fate made her feel more doomed. Kim said a silent prayer and asked God to forgive her for all the things she had done over the years. A feeling of dread and hopelessness crept up on her, and inside her heart, she accepted her impending fate—a long, brutal, and painful death.

Kim could hear her captors arguing now. It was probably about the different ways that they were going to torture and murder her. For a fleeting moment, while still conscious, she started to reflect on her life. She'd always considered that she and Donna had been lucky to make it out of their house alive the night their parents disappeared. She and Donna had the finest material things they could ask for, but she still always felt like she was carrying a big void in her life with the absence of her mother and father.

Kim went through times, like now, when she just wished she'd grown up with a normal life—a mother, a father, regular school, and regular friends. Aunt Lisa wouldn't let them have friends, and she homeschooled them, not on education, but on the art of making a living. Any time Kim and Donna would mention regular kid stuff, Aunt Lisa would shut them right down.

Growing up, Kim had secretly longed to go to high school with normal kids, where she could enjoy sports events, proms, and graduation. Aunt Lisa had brainwashed Kim and Donna to believe that the only friends they needed were one another. Kim had often played the what-if game, and now was no different. *What if our parents had lived? What if Aunt Lisa had never gotten us into catching licks? What if our lives were just regular? What if Aunt Lisa was still alive? What if Donna were here with me now?*

Loud yelling and movement snapped Kim back into her reality.

"Mmmm," she groaned against the gag when she felt rough hands clamp down on her ankles. She couldn't even scream as her body was moved against her will. She was dragged out of the vehicle and hoisted over a man's shoulders, causing terrible pain in her chest and abdomen. She could feel the heat from the sun bearing down on the cuts and bruises on her back.

Kim was in excruciating pain all over her body, but she wasn't going out without a fight. It would be her last-ditch effort to let her captors know that she would not go down easily.

"Mmm! Mmmm!" She tried to scream again, but to no avail. She began bucking her body. Unable to move her bound hands and feet, she used her torso to squirm and try to fight the man carrying her. The pain shooting through her torso almost sent her into shock, but she wasn't stopping.

"Keep still, bitch! I will shoot your ass right here!" the man carrying her barked.

Kim didn't listen. She didn't give a fuck what he was saying, because the way she felt, a quick shot to the head might be welcomed at that moment. She couldn't see herself dying without fighting.

"This little bitch just won't quit," the man growled, annoyed.

Finally, she was thrown down onto what felt like a concrete slab. Her ribs and chest exploded with pain, and she could feel blood leaking like a faucet from her nose.

"Take off the blindfold," she heard a man say in a serene, calm voice.

Kim was barely holding on now. She could feel herself ready to black out. She was roughly dragged up off the floor and made to stand. Her legs could barely hold her up as the bag was snatched from her eyes. One of her eyes was already swollen shut, and her head lolled around, too painful to hold up on her own.

"I've been waiting to get my hands on you and your sister," a strange man said with an evil grin on his lips.

Kim struggled to see him out of her one good eye. She could see that she was standing in the middle of some kind of factory, and it was absolutely freezing.

The man walked over to Kim and back-hand slapped her with all of the power in his body.

"Ugh!" Kim let out a gasp as her body folded to the floor.

"Stand her back up!" the man growled, cracking his knuckles. His goons rushed over and held Kim back up. He hit her again, and then he spit in her battered face. "I've been wanting to do this for years. I take nothing more than pleasure watching you bleed and hurt," the man gritted, hitting her again, this time in her stomach. Urine splashed from Kim's bladder.

"I won't kill her until I take her in front of the sister," the man told his goons, seemingly taking joy in her pain.

"Take her to the other room," he instructed.

Kim was moaning and groaning as she felt like the life was starting to slip from her body. She had never felt that amount of pain in her life.

"Make sure when you get to hell you tell your aunt what she did to you," the man said cruelly.

Tears streamed down Kim's face. Who was this guy? How did he know Kim was at that hotel? Was he following her all this time?

The end was near, and she hadn't gotten a chance to say goodbye to her sister. The last thought on Kim's mind wasn't just her sister, but Keraun. She didn't want to believe he was connected to this. He was the only one who knew where she was going.

Chapter 14

"Donna, are you listening to me? Loyalty is key. Obviously, you and your sister was never taught it," the familiar voice said.

Donna was pushed over until her body crashed violently to the floor. She didn't care anymore. Pain and grief took her into darkness as her mind tried to figure out where it had all gone wrong.

How could I get caught slipping? How could I put us at risk like this? Donna asked herself. She'd been so careful. She'd followed all of Aunt Lisa's road maps and plans to a tee—well, except for veering off to see Black and trusting a stranger. Those were major mistakes. Now she was in this place, and she'd been so badly beaten that she worried she might have brain damage. Details of how she got here were too foggy for her to remember.

"Just tell me who you are," Donna managed, her words coming out in jagged puffs.

"Who am I? I'm your worst nightmare," he gritted, crushing her throat with his huge gorilla hand. Donna's esophagus felt like it had crumbled under his clutch.

"I'm the man your father left for dead when I was loyal to him. I'm the one who deserves to own this city. I am the motherfucker that has spent years looking for all of you—you, your sister, your aunt, and most importantly, Dom and that bitch wife of his," he growled as he squeezed until Donna could no longer breathe.

Had her ears deceived her? That was where she knew him from. The house . . . when she was a kid. In all of her pain, Donna's mind still raced. Hadn't her father and mother been killed? She knew their bodies had never been recovered, but if they were dead, why would this guy still be searching for them? He finally let go of Donna's neck. She began coughing violently and gasping for air.

"I was the boss. I am here for my just due. I never forget, and if your bastard father wants to hide, then he will have to live with y'all dying," the man spat.

Another man rushed over and kicked Donna in the gut, causing her to cough up a mouthful of blood.

"Where is he? Where are they?"

Donna shook her head. She had no idea what this man was talking about. She could feel herself fading. Either death or shock was finally taking over. But then, something she heard brought her back. A name. A familiar name.

"Yo, Big K, come see your handiwork," the man shouted over his shoulder.

Donna's heart sank even further. Even with all the pain wracking her body, nothing hurt her heart more than hearing that Keraun had set them up.

Donna could hear the footsteps getting closer to her. Then she heard his voice. It was confirmation. It was years of trust fading fast. Donna knew now more than ever what real heartbreak was like. She could only imagine what Kim would feel when she saw Keraun there, betraying them. Keraun was the one person, aside from Aunt Lisa, they thought they could trust. Donna had had her doubts here and there, but the doubts were fleeting, and she would've never thought he would stoop this low. Donna knew she and Kim were going to die now. They knew too much. There was no turning back.

"All Lisa had to do was turn them over. She could've saved herself and saved y'all," Keraun said.

His words were like nails on a chalkboard for Donna. She could barely catch her breath.

"I know y'all know where your father and mother are. I found out from Lisa that she knew, and when I tried to get her to tell me, she wouldn't. I know she told y'all," Keraun pressed.

What the hell was he talking about? She felt like she had to be having a bad dream.

"Keraun? How could you this to us? To Kim? I thought you loved her." Donna struggled to get the words out. With that, his evil partner hit Donna again. More blood spilled from her lips. She trembled so hard her bladder leaked. Her insides felt like they were going through a meat grinder.

"No. We don't know," she rasped, her throat feeling like it had a three-alarm fire blazing in it. "No one ever told us anything."

"You do!" Keraun boomed. "Don't be stupid. I know all the things Lisa preached about taking secrets to the grave. I was there, remember, but now is not the time. We ain't fucking around here," Keraun continued.

Donna couldn't believe what was happening. Her parents were alive somewhere? And they had let her and Kim grow up without them? What was she hearing right now?

And Keraun . . . he had gotten so close to Aunt Lisa. He'd spent years acting as if he loved them. He had been a father figure to them . . . all over this. Donna had to hand it to him; he had played his hand very well. He had been patient and took his time. He had acted the part very well. Getting close to Aunt Lisa wasn't an easy task. Keraun had even played them close after Aunt Lisa's murder, acting like he was so concerned about them. He had not only gained their trust; he had become like family.

"Years and years, and we are this close to getting the man that caused us all a lot of strife. When he got away, I knew Lisa knew where he was. It was hard at first. She was one tough bitch, but after a while, she softened to me. She loved me, and in a sick way, I loved her too. All she had to do was give them up. She was so stupid and stubborn," Keraun relayed.

Donna couldn't believe what she was hearing. Her heart broke over and over again. She would've never guessed it. Although at times she was suspicious of Keraun, she always let it go.

"Oh, and all of that stash money, it's ours. There's nothing left for y'all. You know I had never figured Lisa would've shorted me, but I found out a few months back she definitely did. I know y'all thought she was innocent, but she was into a lot of shit, and she rubbed a lot of people the wrong way out in the streets. Too bad she left y'all here to deal with the wrath that was for her." He went on and on.

Donna closed her eyes. How could they all have been so stupid in thinking Keraun could be trusted? How could they have showed him so much love over the years, only to have him turn on them like this? They had all missed it with him. He was a certified snake.

"Now, where the fuck is your father hiding out?" Keraun gritted. "Don't be stupid like Lisa. Give him up and save yourself and Kim. You already know loyalty don't mean shit out here. Don't be stupid."

The only sound she made was a tiny groan. She had given up on life. She was taking one for her family. Fuck it. If she was going to die anyway, she wasn't giving them shit; especially Keraun's traitor ass. Even if Donna believed that her parents were still alive, she wouldn't know the first place to tell them to look.

"He asked you a fucking question!" the other attacker spat. "Answer the fucking question or I'ma make you watch as we take out your sister's teeth, one by one."

"Fu . . . fuck . . . you," Donna said, spitting blood at the man. "Kill us."

The man punched Donna in the top of her head. Sparks of pain exploded through her skull, and she saw fireworks explode behind her eyelids. She gritted against the pain but didn't scream. He slammed his fist into her head again. She couldn't even feel any more pain. Donna began to pray silently that God would just take her life, and Kim's too.

"A'ight, tough girl," Keraun said. "If you're not going to tell us where they are, you've signed your death warrant."

"Kill me, bitch," Donna whispered. "Just . . . fu . . . fuc . . . fucking kill me." She wasn't going to give him the satisfaction of seeing her beg for her life. She wasn't going to scream anymore or cry anymore. She wasn't going to give them anything that they wanted. With the way Donna felt now, she was welcoming death anyway. No Aunt Lisa. No Kim. No mother and father. Nobody. Donna was sure that her face had been permanently damaged, and she didn't want to live with the scars. She just wanted to be put out of her misery once and for all. She knew as vain as Kim had been all of their lives, she would never want to survive if she had to be scarred too.

"Remember, when you go to hell, tell Lisa that you could've saved yourself and Kim and not fail like she did," Keraun gritted.

Donna squeezed her eyes shut tight, waiting for it all to end. She couldn't look over at Kim, because the pain of seeing her die would be too much. Donna steadied her rapid breathing and tried to clear her mind, but all sorts of images from childhood to teenage years, to the licks they'd pulled, suddenly flooded to the forefront of her mind. She thought about the day she got separated from her parents. Her father could've saved them if he'd gotten away, right? She hated him in that moment.

"Why, Daddy?" she murmured.

"One last chance," Keraun snarled. .

Donna knew in that moment she was winning. Even if she died, she would win, because they wanted that information so badly.

Finally, she felt the cold kiss of the gun's metal against the center of her forehead.

BANG! BANG!

Donna had expected to be dead but quickly realized she was alive, and the loud noise wasn't from the gun.

"I suggest you put that shit down, nigga."

Donna opened her eyes in time to see Keraun whirl around and drop his gun at her feet. He looked like he had literally seen a ghost.

There was more commotion as more men trampled into the place. It sounded like a SWAT team, but it was an army of men there to save her. She stretched her eyes wide. Tears of joy drained down her battered cheeks. She sucked in her breath at the sight and knew then that there was a God.

"Donna! Kim!"

She heard their names being called. The voice was familiar, but she had not heard it in so many years, so she couldn't be sure. "Donna! Oh, baby, can you hear me? Are you still with us?"

Donna fought to open her eyes so that she could see the face—a face she didn't think she would ever see again.

Keraun's goons were surrounded now. One false move and they were all going to be laid down in an instant. As messed up as she was, Donna cracked a satisfied smile at the sight.

"Where the fuck did you come from?" Keraun boomed, his face drawn into a tight scowl. "I knew this would draw you out, motherfucker!"

"Just give up, nigga. Ain't no reason for all of this. I'm easy to negotiate with. I didn't come here to kill nobody, I came to get my girls," Dom said forcefully.

Donna couldn't believe her father was alive! After all of these years! She closed her eyes; her injuries were taking over. She just hoped she and Kim could be saved to see another day with their father.

Keraun spit in Dom's direction. "Fuck you! You think it's that easy? You took niggas' whole lives away from them, hid out for years, made us hunt you and them for years, and you think you can just walk back in like nothing?" Keraun barked. His entire body was shaking.

Dom was eerily calm. He really didn't want to shoot everybody in the room, but to save his kids, he would do it. He would do anything.

"I think I'm being fair. You killed my sister-in-law, you have beat my daughters to within an inch of their lives, and I ain't blown your head off yet. Nigga, wake up. Save yourself. You're outgunned," Dom warned, continuing to train his gun on Keraun.

Suddenly, they were both distracted as Tanzi sauntered in, flanked by security.

"Nobody wins when the family feuds, right?" Tanzi said in a smooth voice. She was beautiful. Even all these years later, not one sign of aging showed up on her face or in her body. "This looks like a stupid big-boy fight, and over what? We all lost everything. We all had to rebuild our shit. You killed my sister to find us? Now you've got us here . . . and? We have the backing of every cartel in Mexico, so now what?"

Keraun's jaw rocked like crazy. He felt stupid now. All his years of work down the drain. He was supposed to get the drop on them, not the other way around.

"Now, everyone is going to drop their guns down. You're going to let us take our girls, and you're going to go on with your pathetic life," Tanzi said with feeling.

"Fuck that! I want to see y'all suffer. Y'all not walking out of here that easy!" Keraun barked in response. He was coming completely undone. He was so hell bent on revenge that he didn't even care.

"Nigga, I'll only say it one more time. Take your clowns and go," Dom said with force in his voice. Dom's men began moving in and readying themselves. They didn't take too kindly to people who didn't listen to their boss.

With his chest heaving up and down, Keraun nodded at his goons to release Kim and Donna. "Everybody put their guns down," Keraun demanded.

"Collect them," Dom told his men.

"You killed my sister?" Tanzi asked Keraun straight.

With that, he shifted on his feet slightly. Everyone in the room got uneasy. Keraun was holding his breath.

"And you did this to my children?"

Kim couldn't see out of her eyes, but she could hear the sound of heels clicking against the floors. Kim knew the cadence of that walk anywhere.

"Ma . . . Mama?" Kim croaked through her battered lips.

"I'll ask again. Did you murder my sister?" Tanzi asked Keraun.

"Fuc—" Keraun started.

BANG! BANG! BANG!

Three shots to the head and his body folded to the floor like a sack of potatoes.

"I always take care of the business. Too much talking makes my ass itch," Tanzi said to Dom. He just smiled at her and shook his head. That was why he had loved her so much and so long. She was a real ride or die bitch.

Tanzi rushed over to Kim and Donna. "My babies didn't deserve this. They'd been through enough. My God," she gasped.

Dom knelt next to his wife. "Baby, they are going to be all right. They will have the best of everything, and that's on my life." He held onto Tanzi as she cried.

"Get them some help now! Now!" she barked. The whole place erupted into chaos. Whatever Tanzi wanted, she got it.

Tanzi made sure the doctors their men called could treat her girls without taking them to any hospital. She had to make sure they stayed on the low. They still had enemies after them. They all understood that this was far from over."We can't ever leave them again. They will have to be with us . . . in the business . . . wherever we go," Tanzi told Dom.

"You don't even have to say it. I already know," Dom acquiesced.

"We are going to be a family again. We've missed so much."

"Forever," Dom said.

Tanzi was brought to tears as they prepared to move Donna out past her. She stopped them.

"Hi, love," Tanzi said in a grief-filled voice. "I missed you so much. You're going to be all right."

Donna groaned as tears drained from the sides of her eyes.

"We never have to be apart again. Ever. I promise," Tanzi said with feeling.

"Never again," Donna croaked and then smiled.

"You're going to be okay. We're going to get you some help. You're alive, and we are going to get you some help," one of the doctors said to Kim when he arrived. He reached down and squeezed her hand. Kim didn't know if she was dreaming that she'd seen her parents, or if it was all real.

"Looks like we got here in the nick of time. We are going to save you.""D. . . . Do . . . Donna," Kim rasped.

The doctors looked at each other and avoided looking at Kim. Their facial expressions seemed grave. Kim's heart sank. Dread washed over her. Suddenly, she felt an ache in her soul that was worse than any injuries. She started moving frantically.

"Donna!" Kim managed a scream. She didn't care about her injuries. She was not ready to face the fact that her sister was dead.

"Shhh. Stop. You're going to hurt yourself. Shhh. She's alive, Kim. Donna is alive," Tanzi placated. "We are all here. We are all never going to be separated again," Tanzi said, planting a kiss on Kim's battered head.

Her mother's words were like the sweetest music to Kim's ears. It was music she hadn't heard in years. And Donna was alive!

Finally, Kim closed her eyes and let her body relax against the stretcher. Nothing else mattered, not even the fact that she and Donna would probably still get arrested for Aunt Lisa's murder until they could clear their names.

"You'll get to see your sister once we get you both the treatment you need. With the beatings you both took, you're pretty lucky to still be alive. I guess you're tougher than you look," one of the doctors said.

"How . . . How did you . . . how'd they know we were . . . here," Kim struggled to get her words out.

"Well, they're very powerful people," he replied. They had finally made it to the open back doors of the private ambulance.

"Powerful people get what they want in life," the doctor continued. Then he stepped aside, and Dom stepped from behind him. Kim's heart jerked in her chest, and her battered, swollen eyes went as wide as the swelling would allow.

"Hey, baby girl," Dom said, smiling at his daughter. "Glad you made it out of this shit on the right side of things." He shook his head.

All Kim could do was sob. Seeing her father was like seeing God. "I would've never thought Keraun would turn on me," Kim said.

"In life, baby girl, everything happens for a reason. There was a reason we let y'all grow up without us. We had the end game in mind. Had we come out years ago, we would've never figured out who our real enemies were. It was a major sacrifice getting updates on y'all from Lisa and not being able to be parents to y'all, but in the end, this is how it shook out. I'm just sorry you had to get hurt for it all to end." Dom poured out his heart.

Kim closed her eyes, the exhaustion finally taking over. She could swear it had all been a dream. Everything had played out like something from a movie. It was like one crazy event after another. Tears drained out of her eyes. It was all over now.

"You rest up now, baby girl. I'm back and will protect you with everything I have in my soul," Dom said. "Never forget that. I promise that you'll never have to feel pain again."

"Okay. Let us take her now. We need to get these girls to the spot so they can get immediate medical care. They are pretty messed up," one of the doctors announced. With that, Kim was whisked away.

Donna's deep sleep was interrupted by knocking on the bedroom door.

"Knock, knock," she heard the soft voice of her mother as she opened the room door and tapped at the same time. Donna opened her eyes and noticed her mother's bright smile. It was so comforting after all these years.

"I thought you might want some company," Tanzi said.

Donna smiled, but she also groaned, since moving her body was painful as hell. It had been three days, and she still felt pain like she'd never experienced before.

"I'm sure you'll want to take this visitor," Tanzi assured with a warm smile. Donna exhaled and moved her bandaged head slightly in acquiescence.

Tanzi turned around and called cheerfully to someone behind her,

"Okay, come on in."

Donna stared at the door in rapt anticipation. She was feeling a mixture of fear and eagerness. Finally, she saw the wheels moving through the door. Her insides got warm as the wheelchair was pushed all the way through the doorway.

"Oh my God," Donna gasped. Tears immediately began falling from her eyes in streams. She began crying so hard her bandaged ribs ached.

Kim's face still had the remnants of her assault, but it was just as gorgeous as ever. Those beautiful eyes staring at Donna lit her insides up with warmth. Donna felt like her heart would explode with giddiness.

"Sissy!" Kim yelled. As usual, her infectious smile lit up her gorgeous face.

Donna wished she weren't so restricted by the cast on her legs, because she wanted so badly to jump out of the bed and hold onto her sister and never let go.

"Oh my God," Donna gasped again. It was all she could manage through her sobs of joy.

"Not exactly how we thought this would all end, right?" Kim said as she was pushed right up to the side of Donna's bed.

Donna stretched her hand out toward her sister, and Kim grabbed her hand and brought it up to her face. They both closed their eyes and sobbed with joy.

"I'll never separate from you again. I don't care what happens. We are never going to be apart again," Donna promised.

"Never again, sissy," Kim replied.

With that, Dom and Tanzi walked in and embraced their girls.

"None of us will ever be apart again," Dom repeated.

"Never again," Tanzi followed up.

Kim looked to her mother and asked the question Donna was also thinking: "Why did we have to go through all of this before we could be together?"

"Kim, Donna, we had to do what was right for the family. If we stayed around, trust me, we would all be where my sister is at now. There were a lot of people who didn't want us to grow, and when our power over the streets seemed to be too much, jealousy and greed came into play. There were some attempted hits, but they came up empty.

"We didn't want to leave you, and we sure didn't want to watch you die because someone thought we were alive. Now, we had to be careful, and that's why we left you with your aunt, my sister. She may have seemed really strict and overprotective, but that was for your own good. There were too many variables out there to be relaxed.

"When she told us about you doing licks, we weren't too happy and thought it could bring too much attention, but you guys learned and did your thing. Our enemies were closer than we thought through the years.

"After we heard that Keraun was with y'all, we were happy because he was one of us—at least that's what we thought. Now we know he was actually just going through the motions to get to us, because he wasn't sure if we were dead or in hiding. I don't know who slipped up on giving the idea that we was alive and well, but we will soon find that out too.

"Girls, we knew you went through hell and back from the beginning, but now this is the end, and you will be with us from now on. We will be here to protect you. No more licks, and definitely no more separation. Now we live together as a family."

"Momma, that's all we ever wanted." Kim looked to Donna and smiled.

Also available from

Urban Books

Carl Weber's Kingpins:

Jamaica

by

Racquel Williams

Prologue

Donavan, aka Gaza

"Compound is now open for breakfast," Lieutenant Rodriguez yelled over the loudspeaker.

Fuck. How did I sleep this late? I've waited ten fucking years for this day to come, and my dumb ass fell asleep. I jumped off the top bunk onto the floor. I grabbed my shower bag and rushed toward the shower. To my disappointment, the shower stalls were already packed. Mostly with niggas going to work at Unicor or to the gym for their daily workout routine.

"Damn, homie. This yo' day, ain't it?" my homie Big Cee said to me as we exchanged daps.

"Yeah, you know it, mon. Yo, soon as I touch down, my nigga, I gotcha. You hear me, yo?"

"Man, I already know you got me, bro. Aye, yo, get out there, fuck some bitches, get money, and stay out the motherfucking way. Nigga, I don't want to see you back in here. You heard?" He grabbed me up in a bear-type hug.

"Yo, my nigga, you already know, I'm focused as fuck," I said. "Fuck the Feds. I ain't never coming back to this shit. My nigga, keep yo' head up. You know they passing these laws and shit. Yo' day comin', homie."

"My nigga, I got fifteen bodies on me. Ain't no motherfucking law can get me up out of here unless they drop the motherfucking charges, you dig? All I need you to do is bless a nigga with some change when you send me some pussy pictures. Other than that, go live life, my nigga."

I nodded. "A'ight, man, I got you. I love you, my nigga."

"Yo, lemme go. You know how I hate missing breakfast," he said, trying to hide the tears that were coming down his face. I watched as he ran out of Unit 8H, into the dimly lit federal compound.

I used e'erything in me to fight back tears. Cee was my big homie, my partner up in this bitch. The only nigga that I had confessed a lot of shit to. But he was right; he been down for fifteen years, and the judge had sentenced him to life. E'erybody knew life in prison meant just that: life. The best I could do for homie to show him how much I appreciated him was to keep his books stocked and send him naked bitches. . . .

"Shower open," a dude yelled, interrupting my thoughts.

"Here I come." I squeezed through, not giving a fuck who was next. I was ready to get the fuck up outta here.

"Nigga, how the fuck you goin' to just cut? You see all these motherfuckers waiting to get in," someone said behind me.

I stopped dead in my tracks, then turned around to face the little pussy nigga that had had the balls to say some shit like this to me. I stepped a little closer to his face. "What the fuck you say to me?" I had my fist balled up. Before he could respond, I hit him dead in his mouth. Before I could get another hit in, I felt someone grab my arm.

"Yo, chill out! You goin' to let a bitch-ass nigga take yo' freedom away?" It was Cee holding on to me.

"Nah, bro. Fuck that nigga. I 'on't give a fuck."

"Man, shut the fuck up. Get in the shower, so you can dress and get the fuck up outta here. You in a motherfucking position that myself and other niggas would kill to have." I saw the seriousness in Cee's face, and I knew he meant business.

"A'ight, man." I snatched my arm away and walked into the empty stall.

I was still fuming. But I felt where the big homie was coming from. I had a chance to walk out of here a free man today, and here I was, trying to fight. I cut the shower on, releasing the water on my head. I need to get my mind right before I stepped out today. . . .

Twenty minutes later, I was dressed and ready to go.

"Donavan Coley, to R & D. Donavan Coley, report to R & D."

This was my time, I thought as I strutted to the main building. Niggas were passing by me, giving me daps and reminding me to keep in touch. I assured them I would and kept it pushing.

Freedom at last, I thought.

When average prisoners left prison, they'd either go to a halfway house or go straight home if they maxed out. However, for me, it was different, I was on my way to an immigration holding facility, where I would stay until they shipped me back to my home country of Jamaica.

I was ten years old when Mama and I made our way to the "land of opportunities." Those were my mom's words for the United States. Since I was born and raised in the Kingston slum of McGregor Gully, my destiny was already carved out for me. Mama was a higgler who bought and sold clothes, shoes, and whatever else she could get her hands on to support her five children. There wasn't no Daddy, and the few no-good niggas that came around didn't stick around, especially when it was time to come up off that paper.

After watching Mama struggle by herself for a few years, I decided that I had to go out there and get money by any means necessary. I and two of my partners started hustling weed. The business started off slow, but as time went on, it grew. At first, I was able to help Mama with our food bill. Eventually, I was able to afford more. I remembered the smile on my younger siblings' faces when I bought our first television and brought it home. Then I purchased a nice bed, and before you knew it, our little two-bedroom board house was decked out. I smiled as I thought about the joy on my mama's face. . . .

At some point, a relative of ours in the United States offered to help Mama out. So Mama, my oldest sister, and I came to New York one summer, with no intention of going back to Jamaica. The rest of my siblings remained in Jamaica and lived with my grandmother. Mama quickly married some dude and got her green card in no time. About a year later, my sister and I got ours also.

I wasn't no book-smart nigga, not that I didn't know a little something, but my focus wasn't on that. I wanted to make money fast—not a few dollars, but plenty of them. I started off small, with an eight ball, and worked my way up. At first, things moved slowly for me, because I was the new kid on the block. One night at a club in the Bronx, I met two cats from Jamaica, Leroy and Gio. We became a trio and were inseparable. Whether we were grinding or fucking bitches, if you saw one of us, you saw all of us. It didn't take me long to convince them that we could make this money and start running shit. Later, we made friends with a Trini dude, Demari, who would forever change our lives.

It took me about six years to get shit moving the way I wanted it to move. I found a connect out in Cali to supply me with pure, uncut coke. Within a year we were copping twenty-five kilos on each run. Putting in that work, me

and my crew of five niggas had the East Coast on lock. We
were supplying niggas in Jersey, Delaware, Virginia, and
as far away as Florida. Money was flowing in, and so was
the hate from other niggas. That didn't stop shit, 'cause
after a few altercations and niggas getting dropped, the
word was out there that we were not to be fucked with.
Shit started getting hot, but that didn't deter me and my
crew. Matter of fact, we started going harder at the grind.

I was so caught up in the grind, I was oblivious to the
fact that one of my runners, Demari, had got torn off
in Delaware by the Feds and had decided to rat on me.
What made matters worse was that I had fucked with this
nigga hard. Had brought the nigga to my crib, had gone
on trips with this nigga, and had even bought this nigga
a brand-new Lexus truck. Demari hadn't been moving no
way different, so I had had no reason not to trust him or
believe he was anything short of loyal.

A year later, I was on my way to one of the trap houses
when a black SUV cut me off. I pulled my gun, getting
ready to bust at this clown, before I exited my Range
Rover. Five other black SUVs pulled up. Niggas jumped
out and ran up on me.

"US marshals, get down! Get down!" one of them
shouted.

Fuck! I just shook my head. I thought about trying to
shoot my way out, but I was surrounded. I looked up
and saw a helicopter flying low. It was like in the movies.
These motherfuckers were everywhere. They put the
cuffs on me, and just like that, my life was changed.

As it turned out, all the trap houses were raided, my
niggas were locked up, and accounts were seized. As I sat
in my cell in MDC Brooklyn, I kept wondering how the
fuck the Feds knew so much about my operation. The
answers soon came to me in my motion for discovery.
There was an undercover confidential informant. A

bitch-ass nigga that I fed had crossed me! My lawyer fought, but in the end, the Feds had too much shit on me. From hours and hours of wiretapping, they had amassed a mountain of information about my drug activities and discussions of shootings. My lawyer advised me to go ahead and plead out.

In the end, the judge sentenced me to 180 months in prison, which was equal to fifteen years. I heard Mama screaming out after the sentence was passed down, but I, on the other hand, was feeling blessed. I wasn't happy, but, shit, with all the evidence that they had on me, they could've easily given me life in prison.

I whispered "I love you" to Mama as the marshal led me away. Within weeks I was shipped to Beckley, West Virginia, to do my time. That had been my home for the past thirteen years. Until today . . .

"Let's go, Reid," a marshal yelled, interrupting my deep thoughts.

I opened my eyes and realized the plane had landed. We were in Rhode Island. This was where the immigration prison was located. Mama had told me that the lawyer said I shouldn't be here for nothing over two weeks. But shit, you know how fucked up the system was; these motherfuckers did what the fuck they wanted to do. But fuck it. I done did my time. This shit right here was nothing compared to the shit I had done went through in the pen.

As I exited the plane, I stopped and took a long breath. This shit felt good.

"Move it, Coley," this pussy-ass marshal yelled, as if I was his bitch.

I looked at that nigga, smiled as I kept it pushing. In another lifetime, this nigga would never come out his mouth at me like this. I walked off to the van that they had waiting. We all climbed in and sat there waiting in the hot-ass van, laughing and talking.

"Yo, it's fucking hot in here," a nigga in the back hollered.

But his plea fell on deaf ears. The marshals continued on about their business, ignoring us.

"Yo, pussy. It's hot up in dis van," I yelled.

"What the fuck you just said?" said a white, redneck, bitch-ass nigga as he stepped in the van.

"Nigga, you heard what the fuck I said." I looked that nigga dead in the face. We stared each other down for a good two minutes. This nigga finally backed away. I knew he'd seen in my eyes that there wasn't no bitch in my blood.

Minutes later the other bitch-ass nigga got in the van and pulled off. About thirty minutes later, we arrived at the immigration prison, climbed out of the van, and marched inside. I was eager to get in there, to get a shower, and get something to eat. This small prison was nothing compared to the one I had come from. It was quiet, and I welcomed that. After being in the pen all those years and being around niggas, being in a quieter place was far better. Once you got in bed in the pen, you could never really get a good night's sleep, because niggas were constantly getting killed. You had to be on guard all the time, or you might just be the next victim.

Being the nigga I was, I was always on guard, 'cause I had promised Mama that I would come home to her alive, and not in a body bag, and that was a promise that I could not break. . . .

Chapter One

Gaza

It was surprising how shit had changed in the thirteen years that I'd been gone. I had left Jamaica with Mama and my sister at the age of twenty-two, and here I was, returning at thirty-five, a grown-ass man. I felt kind of funny as I stepped off the United Airlines flight that had taken me from Rhode Island to Kingston, Jamaica. Yes, I was born at Jubilee Hospital and raised in McGregor Gully. When you mentioned the Gully, niggas automatically knew what you were all about. If you were from the Gully, you already knew we were all 'bout our paper. Either we were slinging them rocks, sticking up other dope boys, or pimping bitches out. We were goin' to get it one way or the other. . . .

It was humid as fuck, but it felt good. I stood outside, inhaling and exhaling the air on this hot August day. I looked around me; nothing seemed familiar. The last time I was here, in my country, I was a little-ass young man. I ain't goin' to lie: I started feeling crazy as fuck. I felt everyone was staring at me. I knew they were aware that this was the plane that carried the deportees.

After going through customs, I finally walked out the door. People were everywhere, and cars were pulling up to the curb. I felt like I wanted to run back inside the terminal, hide from all this chaos around me. . . .

"Donavan." I heard someone yellin' my government. I immediately recognized the voice without seeing the face.

I looked at the crowd of people that were standing around, and there was my mama, my queen, waving at me. I smiled and pushed through the crowd, trying to get to her.

"Oh my God. My baby is free!" she screamed as she hugged me. Then she started planting kisses on my forehead.

Seconds later a car pulled up, and dude started honking his horn at us.

"Go the fuck around. You see me hugging ma child," Mama said and flicked the man a bird.

"Come on, Mama. 'Cause if him, that pussy, say anything to you, it's gonna be bloodshed out here today." I was so serious, and I let it be known.

She finally let me go out of her tight embrace, pointed to her car, and climbed behind the wheel. I threw the envelopes that I had in my possession on the backseat and then got in the front passenger seat. Mama pulled off, still cussing the man out with her raw Jamaican accent, which seemed to get stronger the older she got.

"Damn, Ma. Ain't nothing change. You still a gangsta," I joked.

"Baby, don't yuh start, now. You know yuh mama can handle herself."

Her ass was nothing but about four feet five, but you couldn't tell by her voice, which was strong whenever she spoke. Mama was the type to whup on niggas and bitches. I remembered how she used to beat this nigga Tony that she used to fuck with back when we lived in Jamaica. I mean, Mama used to use a broomstick on that nigga. It was funny as hell, because this nigga was big and bulky. He used to run out of the house, yelling cusswords until he got outside the gate. Thinking back on those good old days, I couldn't help bursting into laughter.

"What the hell so funny, boy?"

"Ma, you remember how you used to run after Tony, hitting him with a broomstick and shit?"

"That damn fool Tony. You know he got killed a few years back? Gunmen ran up in his house in Portmore and killed him and his son. Word had it, him and his son was wrapped up in that scamming thing."

"Really? That's fucked up."

"Boy, watch yo' damn mout'," she said with her raw Jamaican accent.

"My bad, Mama, but you do know I'm thirty-five years old now, right?"

She swung that neck around so fast and looked at me. "And what's that supposed to mean?"

"Just easy yo' self. You done know how do things set already."

"Uh-huh. So how it feel to be among the free?"

"You know, I don't really feel it as yet. Ask mi dis same question in about a month."

"Well, I'm just happy you are here. I pray night and day fi God to let you come home to me safe and sound. And here you are, my baby," she said.

"You done know mi a God bless and Father God not leaving my side."

"Well, everybody is at the house, waiting fa you. They are so happy you home."

"Oh yeah." I smiled.

It had been thirteen years since I'd seen my family. As I said, my mom, my oldest sister, and I were the only ones that had made it to the United States. The rest of my family had stayed in Jamaica, with my grandmother. I was really excited just to be in the presence of people that I knew genuinely loved me. . . .

I watched as Mama pulled up at a gate outside the three-story crib that my money had helped build after we left Jamaica. This was one of the first things I had done when I started making money in New York. I was as proud of it as I was of the big house in New York that I had bought Mama. When the Feds had got me, they couldn't touch neither house, 'cause Mama worked, had money in the bank, and had the houses in her name, and they couldn't prove she knew anything about my illegal activities. My mama wasn't no fool, and she handled her shit like a real G.

"Oh shit! This is it, Mama?" I said as she punched the code in the keypad. She waited for the gate to open and then drove up the marble driveway.

"Yes, son, this is it," she answered as the gate swung shut behind us.

After she stopped the car and turned off the ignition, I stepped out of the car and just stood there, looking. This house was more beautiful in person than it was in the pictures I had seen.

"Gaza is here," I heard one of brothers yell.

All I saw out of the corner of my eye was people rushing out of the house. Not just any people, though. Familiar faces ran up to me and almost knocked me to the ground.

"What's good, family?" said the same brother who had announced my arrival. He hugged me tight. See, this was the brother that I was closest to, and he was the one that everybody said was my twin. We hugged for a good minute before my grandma interrupted.

"Mi grandbaby. Come give yo' grandmother a big hug." She pushed my brother out of the way.

"Grandma Rosie, what a gwaan?" I tried to use my rawest patois on her.

"Welcome home, mi baby. Come. I know you must hungry." She took my hand and led me into the house. That didn't stop everyone else from following behind us. The treatment that I was getting was nothing short of that afforded royalty.

My grandma ushered me into the dining room. On the long table were large bowls of curry goat, white rice, oxtails, and jerk chicken, as well as a big jar of sorrel punch. Wait, it wasn't even Christmastime, and sorrel was being served. I smiled as I looked at the family members surrounding me. This was the place I need to be, among real family. . . .

***

It was a little after 11:00 p.m., and all the festivities had died down. I kissed Grandma on the cheek after she gave me a very serious tongue-lashing about my troubles with the law. I guessed this was long overdue.

I walked out on the balcony, with a Guinness in hand, and rolled me a blunt. I welcomed this serene feeling I was experiencing right now. I took a long drag of the weed and instantly started to choke. I mean, a nigga ain't smoked in a few years. When I first got to the pen, me and one of my cellies used to hustle the weed inside. But just as on the outside, niggas started snitching. After my cellie got caught and more time was added to the twenty years he was doing, I decided to chill out. My black ass was trying to come up out of there, not add a single day to what that bitch-ass judge had done gave me.

The house was up in the hills of Cherry Gardens and overlooked the entire downtown. The view was spectacular to a nigga that had had to look at brick buildings for over a decade. I sipped on the Guinness, took a few more pulls, being careful not to choke.

"Yo, Father, what's the pree?" said a male voice behind me.

"Oh shit! My nigga," I exclaimed as I turned around.

It was my right-hand man, Gio. He was my partner from back in the day, had run with me in New York.

"Yo, Father, how freedom feel?"

"Feel motherfucking good. This is what I been waitin' on." I looked around, inhaling the fresh Jamaican air.

"Welcome home, nigga." He gave me dap; then he handed me a key fob and a cell phone.

"What's this, yo?" I shot him a suspicious look.

"Go out front and see fa yourself."

He walked back inside the house, made his way to the foyer, went out the front door, and headed down the steps to the driveway. I followed him. Outside of the crib sat a black BMW with rims. I walked over to it and stared at the beauty.

"This is your ride. Welcome home, Father," Gio said.

I looked at him to see if this was a big joke, but he stood there, with a serious look plastered all over his face. I looked down at the key fob in my hand, didn't see a key. "Yo, where's the key?"

"Oh shit. I forgot you been gone for a minute. This a keyless, push-button car. Yo, we don't drive vehicles if they not push button. Press the button on the fob and open it up."

This was dope as shit. I looked down at the key fob, pressed the UNLOCK button. I then opened the car door, climbed in, and pressed the START button. Nothing. "Yo, what the hell? Why it ain't starting?"

He leaned in the car. "Put yo' foot 'pon the brake pedal."

He then pushed the button. The car started. Yo, this was new to me. I hadn't driven in years, but I was eager to test out my new whip.

"Hop in, nigga," I told him.

He jumped in on the passenger side, and I pulled off. The ride started off a little rough, 'cause this baby had power and a nigga was rusty, but I quickly got it under control. I went around the block a few times, catching the stares of bitches and niggas that were hanging out late. Then we went back to the house, and we drank a bottle of Patrón that he had brought over and smoked blunts back-to-back on the balcony. It felt good to have in my presence one of my niggas who had been rolling with me from day one. It was a little after 5:00 a.m. when he rolled out and I left the balcony and went back into the house. I took a quick shower before going into my bedroom. It felt so good to be in a real bed, and not on that cot they had in jail. Before I knew it, a nigga was out. . . .

***

I heard banging on the bedroom door, which woke me up out of my sleep. I jumped up, looked around. That was when I realized I wasn't in prison. I had been in a deep sleep when the knocking startled me. . . .

"Donavan, you still sleeping?" Mama's voice echoed through the crack in the door.

Oh shit. I had forgotten she was leaving, was going back to the States today. I was supposed to take her to the airport. I grabbed my phone and looked at the time. It was well after 12:00 p.m. "I'm up, Mama. Give me a few minutes."

I rushed to the bathroom, took a quick shower, and grabbed one of the white T-shirts and jean shorts Mama had brought down for me. In no time, I was dressed and ready to go. I walked in the kitchen, where my grandma was sitting with an older-looking woman.

"Doris, this is the man of the house, Donavan. He will be your new boss."

Doris stood, walked over to me, and shook my hand. "Nice to meet you, young man. I hear all good things 'bout you."

"Nice to meet you too, Miss Doris."

My mother walked in just then. "Your breakfast is on the dining-room table," she said.

"Thanks, Mama, but I'm ready to take you to the airport."

"Donavon, is who car parked out in the front?" my mother asked.

"It's mine, Mama."

"Is yours?" She stopped dead in her tracks, turned around, and looked at me.

That lady's look had never changed over the years. Whenever she was displeased with any one of us, she had a special look that she would shoot our way. This time was no different, but the only thing was, I was no longer a little boy and I wasn't afraid to face her.

"You late, right? You 'on't wanna miss that flight," I reminded her.

I left the kitchen, grabbed her bags in the foyer, carried them out, and then placed them in the trunk of the car. I got behind the wheel and waited for her. She finally appeared and got in the passenger seat, and then we drove off. I could tell she was feeling some type of way, 'cause her mood had changed drastically.

"Donavan . . . I know you're grown and I can't tell you how to live ya life, but Jamaica is not a nice place. You left here when you was a young man. Now it's more killing. Don't come down here and get wrap up with these bwoy down here."

"Mama, listen, you need to stop worrying. I'm good, trust me."

"You betta be, 'cause I don't want to lose you. Don't you trust none of these people down yah. You been gone too damn long to come down yah and lose your life."

"Mama, come on. You worry too much, mon. Relax. I want you fi go home and focus on enjoying life. Trust me, I got this."

"All right. Me warning you. My mother always say, 'A hard head make a soft ass.'"

I burst out laughing. "Mama, you have always said the same thing too."

She didn't respond; instead, she turned her head and stared out the window. I cut on the music to kind of mellow out the mood.

When we reached the airport, I pulled over to the curb and unloaded Mama's luggage. When she got out of the car, I turned to her and said, "I love you, Mama." I hugged her tight as she professed her love for me and repeated that these people were no good.

Then I watched as she strutted into the airport terminal. When she looked back, I waved one last time. After she had disappeared inside the terminal, I hopped back in the car and pulled off.